SKELETON CREEK
THE PHANTOM ROOM

By Patrick Carman

The Crossbones

My name is Ryan McCray and I'm a member of a secret society. It's called the Crossbones. There are a grand total of three members: me, Sarah Fincher, and Sam Fitzsimmons.

Ryan, Sarah, and Fitz.

I know it sounds like a big organization with offices in Switzerland and Zurich and thousands of members worldwide. But that's it, just the three of us. And we like it that way.

Sarah is my best friend and Fitz runs a close second. We live in the dead end town of Skeleton Creek and we have a knack for finding trouble. Or maybe it has a way of finding us, I can't really tell anymore. Sarah lives on one end of town, I live on the other, and Fitz lives in the suburbs.

Har har har. I made myself laugh right there.

I can throw a rock from my front yard

and nearly hit Sarah's house. Skeleton Creek is that small. So the suburbs of Skeleton Creek are approximately six double wide trailers and a few cabins sprinkled through the woods in a five mile radius. Fitz's dad has a trailer in the burbs, but he also owns a house a block off of Main Street. Apparently he never uses it.

Fitz was a no show for the last Crossbones meeting. He also hasn't been online or on his phone. He hasn't shown up for work at my dad's fly shop. No sign of his motorbike spewing a gray-blue stream of smoke we can always see coming. Two days and no sign of Fitz. Not a word.

So Sarah and I went looking. Because that's what we do. We investigate things when they don't seem right. And Fitz disappearing for two days was not right.

We went by his dad's trailer, hoping

TO FIND SOME SIGN THAT THEY'D GONE ON A FISHING OR HUNTING TRIP. THE TRAILER LOOKED LIKE IT HAD BEEN BOARDED UP AND LEFT FOR DEAD.

"THAT'S WEIRD," SARAH SAID. "LOOKS LIKE NO ONE HAS BEEN AROUND FOR DAYS."

SHE TRIED TO TURN THE HANDLE ON THE FRONT DOOR AND FOUND THAT IT WAS LOCKED.

"DO THEY REALLY THINK SOMEONE IS GOING TO ROB THIS PLACE?" SHE ASKED, SHAKING HER HEAD. "NOT LIKELY."

"LET'S TRY IN TOWN," I SAID. "THE LAST THING WE NEED IS FITZ'S SCARY DAD SHOWING UP. I'M NOT ARMED."

"I AM," SARAH SAID. SHE PULLED HER VIDEO CAMERA OUT AND STARTED SHOOTING THE TRAILER. THAT WAS SARAH: ALWAYS FILMING, EVEN IF THERE WASN'T AN OBVIOUS REASON FOR IT.

"WHAT USE IS THERE FOR FOOTAGE OF A DOUBLE WIDE TRAILER IN THE WOODS?" I ASKED, WISHING WE COULD JUST LEAVE. THE PLACE WAS GIVING ME THE CHILLS.

"Maybe I'm making a documentary on trailers," she said, and I couldn't tell if she was joking or not. "Like a coffee table book with pictures of old trains or boats. Only this would be a collection of videos on YouTube."

"A collection of videos about crummy trailers?" I asked. "You really think people are going to watch that?"

She took her eye away from the viewfinder.

"Maybe if we put kittens on the roof," she said, mulling the idea. "I'll edit them in later."

I started to walk away because sometimes Sarah will only stop shooting if I start moving. This was one of those times. She followed along, still trying to get a few more seconds of footage, and it was like we were attached with a string as she back peddled towards me.

"It's getting close to dark," I said. "Maybe we should tell someone we can't find him."

"Do you know where the house is? The one his dad owns in town but never stays in?"

"Yeah, I think so," I said. I'd only been there once over a year ago.

"Let's try there first, just in case," Sarah said. "Maybe he just needs some space after the whole thing with his dad."

As we walked back towards town on a winding gravel road, I thought about what Sarah had said. The Crossbones had been around a long time, long before we ever became a part of it. We'd uncovered it for what it was: a group of people dedicated to protecting secrets from the past. It's always been a little murky what they were protecting for sure, but the important part is that Fitz's dad was a member of the Crossbones.

"Fitz's dad did seem to take the end kind of hard," I said. "And he's a scary dude. I'm glad he's scarce around town."

Sarah nodded. Me, Sarah, Fitz – we had taken the place of the old Crossbones. Their time was in the past, ours was now. And it was our job to figure out what they'd really been hiding. What was that old group up to? It couldn't have only been about protecting freedom and getting rid of our enemies, as we'd been told. Something else was lurking in the shadows of the Crossbones. I could feel it.

We found the house and walked up to the door. The porch light was on, a good sign, and the house itself seemed to be in good shape. It looked like someone had been taking care of the yard, maybe even living there.

"It's a big place for one guy," Sarah said, looking up at the second story. "I wonder why they have two places?"

I knocked on the door and even turned the handle without waiting very long. The door was locked, no sound came from the inside.

"Let's go around back," Sarah said. This was exactly what I expected her to say. Sarah was born to investigate. I was born to write and read, but investigating is growing on me.

"You're not going to like what's back there," I said.

"Are you trying to scare me, Ryan McCray?"

We rounded the corner and found an iron fence that ran the length of the backyard. It kept going into the darkness on both sides. What lay on the other side was a place I wanted no part of: the Skeleton Creek cemetery.

"Oh right," Sarah said, looking around to get her bearings as night approached. "This house backs up against the old cemetery."

"Maybe that's why he doesn't like being here," I said.

"And why it was probably so cheap."

I yelled Fitz's name into the graveyard, but there was no answer. It was bigger than it should have been for how small the town was, but it was also the only cemetery for many miles and always had been. People had been buried in there for hundreds of years.

Sarah went to the back door of the house and didn't bother knocking.

"Hey, it's not locked," she said.

"Don't open that," I tried to say as fast as I could, but it wasn't fast enough. A tiny dog ran through the crack and headed for the fence.

"Stop it!" Sarah yelled.

But this was a very fast ball of fur. I reached down to grab the dog and it darted through my legs. A second later it was through the fence gap and running into the darkness.

"Way to go, dog whisperer," Sarah said.

"Why'd you have to open that

door?" I asked. I took a deep breath. "Come on. We have to walk into a cemetery at night and find Fitz's dog."

"Fitz has a dog?" Sarah asked as she came up beside me.

I shrugged. "I guess it comes with the house."

The Clause

Sarah and I found Fitz sitting on a tombstone. He was bigger than I was by about thirty pounds. We'd met on the football team, where we both rode the bench for one year. He was wearing black jeans, a red hat, and a T-shirt with a cartoon duck on it. These were bad signs. He'd told me before: red hats and black pants ward off spirits (where he heard this I have no idea), and the cartoon duck was there to keep him company. This was Fitz's 'I need to be alone' outfit.

"Hey, Fitz," I said, trying to keep

things chill. "What's up?"

"Seriously, Fitz, what gives?" Sarah started in. She'd let her dark hair grow even longer than usual and it fell down over one of her eyes as she sat on a tombstone next to our buddy.

"He'll talk to us when he's ready to," I said.

Sarah was always the one to dive right in, but I felt like Fitz needed some space. We needed to coax him out of his shell like a hermit crab.

"Come on, Fitz. Spill it," Sarah said. "What's eating you? And where have you been?"

I rolled my eyes — wow Sarah, way to go in like a bulldozer.

Fitz looked up at me. He was a kind looking guy, with floppy hair and a round face. He looked scared.

"Sorry I went all quiet," he finally said. "It's been a weird time."

"Weird how?" Sarah pressed.

Fitz got up like he was going to wander off on his own.

"We're your friends, Fitz," I said. "If you're in some sort of trouble, maybe we can help."

"We're more than friends. We're the Crossbones," Sarah added. "We don't keep things from each other."

That seemed to get Fitz's attention and he looked at us both.

"This isn't the kind of stuff you can go off and tell your parents. You gotta keep it secret."

Sarah eyed me with a nod. The look we gave each other said it all: we were secret keepers, always had been.

"Please say you didn't murder someone," Sarah said. "I'd rather not be an accessory to a crime."

Fitz smiled briefly and looked out across the many tombstones. There had to be a thousand of them.

"My dad's gone. Not sure he's coming

back," Fitz said.

"Dang, that's rough," I said. Fitz's mom had been dead a long time, both Sarah and I knew that. I couldn't imagine being without my mom and my dad.

"What makes you say that?" Sarah asked. "Of course he's coming back."

Fitz shrugged, kicked the dirt.

"He's been gone for days on end before, usually out in the woods. He's such a mountain man, he can't help it. This time's different. He's been gone for almost two weeks."

"That is a long time," Sarah said. "Maybe he's tracking a bear or a mountain lion."

"I'm old enough to take care of myself," Fitz said. "I have a job and a house. I know how to make pancakes. What else do I need anyway?"

Sarah reached an arm around his shoulder and pulled him in close. "You need us. We're the Crossbones. We don't go it alone, got it?"

Fitz smiled a little more. "Yeah, I get it."

I asked: "Why do you think he left this time? Do you think it had anything to do with us?"

Fitz sighed and shook his head. "I don't know, maybe. I think he was hiding something all those years and just couldn't take it anymore. And we did invoke The Clause. We sort of kicked him out of his own club."

The Clause. Fitz had said it to his dad. It went like this:

We believe in the everlasting supremacy of one generation after another.
We believe that the world is ever changing.
We give power to the first born son of the last man standing.
We trust in the passing of time and the knowing of all things.

The duty to preserve falls now in the line of all good men.

I take this oath
To preserve Freedom
To maintain secrecy
To destroy all enemies

I appoint these three:

To Protect: Sam Fitzsimons
To Record: Sarah Fincher
To Treasure: Ryan McCray
We are the Crossbones now.

The Clause sounds important because it is. It has real weight. When you say it, it has power. And Fitz had said it to the last living Crossbones member: his own dad. He'd released his dad from service, to what we still didn't know.

"Maybe your dad just needs some time to get used to the new

arrangement," Sarah said.

Fitz didn't buy it.

"We were never close and now he's gone," Fitz said. "Even before my mom died, he was always out in the woods or off thinking somewhere."

I looked back in the direction of the house we'd come from.

"How come you have a trailer and a house?" I asked.

"The trailer is my dad's. He had it before he met my mom. But the house was hers."

I wondered but didn't ask why they hadn't chosen to live in town. It was obvious Fitz's dad liked it better the closer he was to the wild. He wouldn't have wanted to live in Skeleton Creek if he didn't have to.

"Let's go back to your house, Fitz," Sarah said. "I'm in the mood for a pancake."

"Can't go back, not yet."

That was odd. I looked at him with a questioning stare that cut through the darkness.

"The place is haunted," Fitz finally said. He started defending himself before we could say another word. "I know it sounds crazy, but I'm telling you, it is. It's why we never stayed there. But I'm staying there now."

"Heck yeah!" Sarah said. "And here I thought Skeleton Creek was about to get boring! This is awesome."

"Awesome?" Fitz asked.

"Of course it is! Think of all the stuff we get to investigate now. Fitz, you saved us."

Fitz looked at me like Sarah had gone crazy.

"Just go with it man, you'll get used to this," I said.

Sarah was pacing back and forth in serious thought mode.

"You guys, we're the Crossbones.

This is what we do. It's what we've always done. I can feel it. This is the beginning of something big."

I wasn't even close to convinced.

"You said you couldn't go back to the house yet," I said. "What did you mean?"

Fitz glanced at his watch. "I can go back in 92 minutes."

Sarah was very interested in this piece of information.

"Why 92 minutes?" She loaded her camera onto her shoulder and got ready to film the answer.

"I'd really rather you didn't record this," Fitz said. "I don't like being on camera."

"Join the club," Sarah said. "Neither do I."

But she kept filming anyway.

"Right now it's just past nine o'clock," Fitz went on. "At 10:07 stuff starts happening in my mom's old room.

It's safe to go back in there at 10:30."

He looked at his watch once more. "That's 91 minutes from now."

I took a couple of steps towards Fitz. So did Sarah.

And then I asked him:

"What kind of stuff?"

Steve gets us into a tight spot

Fitz put his hands in his pockets and turned away from us. I knew him well enough to know what this meant: he was nervous.

"It's okay," I said. "You can trust us. We're not going to tell anyone."

He looked into Sarah's camera.

"Could you please turn that thing off? I don't want this recorded."

Sarah reluctantly let the camera drop from her eye.

"Fine."

Fitz and I both looked at her.

"You didn't turn it off, did you?" I

asked.

We knew Sarah was good at shooting from the hip. She'd done it plenty of times before.

"Okay, okay," she grumbled, tapping the stop button. "Don't come crying to me when we wish we had the whole story on tape for posterity."

Fitz rubbed his hands on his pant legs nervously. "Everything you guys have ever investigated has turned out to be false. But I'm telling you guys, this is real. It's different."

"What's real?" I asked.

I couldn't help thinking about how haunted the dredge had seemed before we unraveled its mysteries. And Old Joe Bush. There was a time in my life when I would have said that dude was a real ghost, no doubt about it. But we'd always kept digging until the truth was uncovered. And the truth never included a real ghost.

"It always starts at 10:07PM," Fitz began. "There's a voice. It whispers. Sounds like it's coming out of the walls."

"What does it say?" Sarah asked. I could tell it was killing her not to push that record button.

"Same thing every time. Just one word, over and over: Sid."

"Sid? Sounds like a name to me," I said.

"And that's not all," Fitz said. He could see we weren't going to make fun of him or try to debunk anything. He was more excited to talk. "There's also another sound, like someone is moving in the room."

"This is so cool," Sarah said, her trigger finger on the record button.

"Don't do it," I warned her.

"And the door to my room opens and closes on its own. Sometimes it slams shut."

"Whoa," I said. Now I was starting to get pumped, too. "Fitz, this could be a real live haunting."

Fitz looked at me quizzically. "Wait, you mean you believe me?"

"Of course we believe you, don't we Sarah? Sarah?"

Sarah had started walking away.

"Where's she going?" Fitz asked.

I knew exactly where she was headed, but I asked her anyway.

"Hey! Where to in such a hurry?"

Sarah turned back just long enough to tell me what I already knew.

"If we go now, I can set up a camera in there before 10:07PM."

I looked back and Fitz and wondered what he was thinking. He'd gone totally white, all the blood running out of his face.

"I'm not sure I can go back in there," he said.

"You don't have to," Sarah called

back. "I'll take care of everything."

She took a few more steps and stopped suddenly. In the pale moonlight I could see she'd remembered something important.

"We might have let your dog out," Sarah said. "Oops."

"You let Steve out of the house?!" Fitz practically yelled. "Ah man."

"Steve?" I said. I didn't even know Fitz had a dog. "Who names a dog Steve?"

Fitz started walking deeper into the cemetery, away from his house.

"I just got him at the pound down in Baker City. Steve doesn't know his way around. The little guy is lost!"

Sarah looked towards the house longingly, but I knew we had to find the dog first.

"If you want to go set up your camera, we can find...Steve," I said.

I didn't think for a second Sarah would go into a potentially haunted house by herself, but she was so psyched for ghost action there was no stopping her.

"Try to get back to the house by 10:07," she said. "I'll set it up so we can record without having to be in the house."

She took off before I could answer and I double timed it to catch up with Fitz.

"She's even braver than I thought," Fitz said. "Impressive."

"You have no idea," I agreed. Then I yelled for the dog.

"Hey, cool it Ryan. Keep it down."

I had no idea why we had to keep it down, but Fitz quickly explained.

"There's a big guy out here, this African American dude. He's like a giant, takes care of the cemetery."

"I know about him," I said. "He never

talks to anyone. And you're right. He's gigantic."

"That's the guy. Anyway he caught me out here a few nights ago and told me to stay out of the cemetery at night."

We moved slowly, whispering Steve's name.

"Why'd you name your dog Steve?" I asked.

Fitz shrugged. "Never had a brother and I always liked the name Steve. It seems friendly."

"Fair enough."

After awhile we arrived at the crypt yard, which was surrounded by concrete walls. We were standing at the farthest end of the cemetery, closest to Skeleton Creek.

"The water runs underground, too," Fitz said. "I guess people liked to be buried above ground on this end of the graveyard. They also liked it closest

TO THE WATER."

"THERE'S SOMETHING ABOUT AN ABOVE GROUND TOMB THAT FREAKS ME OUT," I SAID. WE BOTH STARED UP AT THE WALLS SURROUNDING THE CRYPT YARD. AND THEN WE HEARD IT.

"UH OH," I SAID.

THE SOUND OF A SMALL DOG, YIPPING FROM INSIDE THE WALLS.

"HOW THE HECK DID STEVE GET IN THERE?" I ASKED.

"THERE," FITZ ANSWERED. THE LIGHT WAS VERY FAINT, BUT I COULD SEE THE SMALL OPENINGS ALONG THE BOTTOM OF THE WALL. NOT BIG ENOUGH FOR ME OR FITZ TO FIT THROUGH, BUT PLENTY BIG FOR A TINY DOG.

"YOU GOTTA BE KIDDING ME," I SAID.

"MAYBE IF WE CALL IT WILL COME BACK OUT?" FITZ WONDERED ALOUD.

WE CALLED IN A QUIET WHISPER, BUT STEVE WAS EITHER CONFUSED OR DIDN'T WANT TO COME WHEN HE WAS CALLED.

"DOES HE KNOW HIS NAME?" I ASKED.

"Kind of. Maybe. Actually no."

"Fitz, when did you get this dog?"

Fitz looked at the ground like he didn't want to say. Steve barked from behind the wall.

"I took my dad's old truck into Baker City for supplies this afternoon."

"And you came back with Steve," I continued.

"That's pretty much the deal, yeah." No wonder Steve wouldn't come when we called him.

I moved in for a closer look at the crypt walls. There was only one door in and of course it was locked, but there were notches in the corners of the walls where I could put my feet. They ran all the way to the top.

"I'll catch you if you fall," Fitz said.

"Gee, thanks big guy."

As I got started I had to admit this was just like every other time I'd gotten myself into trouble. Here I was in a cemetery at night, climbing the walls of a crypt yard.

No wonder my parents don't trust me.

I was at the top in a few seconds, looking down into a space that was about as big as a tennis court, only it was square.

"Whoa," I said. "This is crazy in here. It's been awhile."

I'd seen it before, but it was daylight and the door had been open. Sarah and I had snuck in to check it out when we were 11 or 12. Looking down on it now, all cast in moonlight and shadow, it looked like an ancient city of old buildings.

"Do you see Steve?" Fitz asked. I didn't.

"Going down," I said, and began climbing down the other side.

Walking around inside a crypt yard

after dark is about as scary as being inside the dredge at midnight. So many shadows, so many bodies above ground in stone chambers. Chilling to say the least.

"Steve," I called quietly. "Here boy."

Something moved out in the crypt yard and a shadow darted to my left. My legs moved like thick oatmeal, slowly, one foot in front of the other, until I was in the very center of the enclosed space. I felt like I was in a city of stone, waiting for a full on zombie attack.

I saw the shadow move again, and this time I moved faster. This turned out to be a mistake, because while I did see Steve for a brief second, my sudden movement scared him right through one of those small holes at the base of the wall.

For some reason I felt even worse than I had before.

Now I truly was alone in the crypt yard. Even Steve had left me.

"Fitz!" I yelled. "He ran out on your left side!"

"Okay!" Fitz yelled back.

I assumed he was gone, taking chase, and started for the wall.

That's when I realized something about the crypt yard that I should have seen before I climbed down. On the way in, I basically dropped until my arms hung from the wall, then let go and fell the extra few feet. But now, as I looked for the same notches I used as hand holds to get in, I saw that there was no such help on this side.

My phone buzzed in my pocket.

A text from Sarah.

You guys need to get over here like yesterday. Where are you?!

I texted back, because it took my mind

OFF OF BEING TRAPPED IN A CEMETERY.

TIED UP AT THE MOMENT, HEADING BACK SOON.

I WENT TO THE ONE DOOR AND HOPED IT WOULD OPEN, BUT FOUND THAT IT WAS DEAD BOLTED SHUT. THERE WAS NO MECHANISM TO OPEN IT FROM EITHER SIDE. A PERSON NEEDED A KEY TO OPEN THIS DOOR.

BUZZ.

ANOTHER TEXT FROM SARAH.

I'M ALL SET UP. IF THIS IS HAPPENING, IT WILL BE SOON. GET BACK HERE!

I TEXTED BACK.

ACTUALLY, IF YOU WOULDN'T MIND, COULD YOU GET A ROPE FROM FITZ'S GARAGE AND COME RESCUE ME? I'M TRAPPED IN THE CRYPT YARD.

MY TEXTS HAVE BEEN RUNNING A LITTLE

long sometimes lately. I consider it practice for when I write my novel.

A long pause and no answer from Sarah. I sent her another text. This one was much shorter.

Hello?

Still no answer and it seems like Fitz has left the country searching for Steve.

Why me?

Roy Web

The clock on my phone clicks to a time I really wish it would skip altogether. But like all great horror movies, my phone will not skip the best parts.

10:07PM.

I have to imagine Sarah is not coming to save me. She's too busy freaking out over potential ghostly footage. It's right when I was thinking this

THOUGHT THAT I HEARD A KEY BEING INSERTED INTO THE WOODEN DOOR AT THE OTHER END OF THE CRYPT YARD. IT SOUNDED LIKE A REALLY BIG KEY.

I HID BEHIND ONE OF THE WIDE CRYPTS AND FELT MY HEART BEATING OUT OF MY CHEST. WHATEVER KIND OF LATCH WAS ON THAT DOOR, IT MUST HAVE BEEN HALFWAY RUSTED SHUT. WHEN THE LOCK TURNED IT MADE A GRATING SOUND OF METAL ON METAL. AND THEN THE HEAVY DOOR WAS FLUNG OPEN. WHOEVER WAS STANDING IN THE DARKNESS WAS ALMOST AS BIG AS THE OPENING ITSELF. IT LOOKED LIKE THE SHADOW OF A GIANT WHO HAD COME TO PICK ME UP AND CARRY ME AWAY INTO THE FOREST. HAD SASQUATCH FINALLY FOUND ME? I KNEW THAT THING WAS REAL!

THEN I HEARD THE BARK OF A SMALL DOG.

"THIS LITTLE GUY BELONG TO YOU?"

THE VOICE WAS DEEP AND SLOW AND FULL OF SOUTHERN DRAWL.

I DIDN'T ANSWER, SO THE GIANT MOVED FORWARD, CASTING HIS INHUMANLY LARGE SHADOW OVER THE CRYPT YARD.

"I KNOW YOU'RE IN HERE. YOU'RE BUDDY TOLD ME."

"FITZ?" I SAID.

"RYAN?! HEY RYAN! I'M RIGHT HERE MAN!"

"HOW COME YOU'RE SO HUGE?"

I THOUGHT THE DARKNESS MUST HAVE BEEN PLAYING TRICKS ON ME. HOW DID FITZ GET TWO TIMES HIS ALREADY LARGE SIZE? AND WHY WAS HIS VOICE SO LOW AND SLOW AND SOUTHERN?

"OH, SORRY MAN," HE SAID.

A SECOND SHADOW APPEARED. FITZ.

"COME ON OUT, RYAN. IT'S COOL."

IT DIDN'T LOOK COOL, I CAN TELL YOU THAT. BUT WHAT WAS I GOING TO DO? I'D ALREADY BEEN TRAPPED WITH A BUNCH OF DEAD PEOPLE A LOT LONGER THAN I'D WANTED TO BE. I STOOD UP AND WALKED OUT INTO THE OPEN TO MEET MY MAKER.

As I got closer, I saw that Fitz was standing next to the biggest man I'd ever met in person. His face was dark, with giant round eyes that matched his round head. He was totally bald, and the top of his head shone with the light of the moon.

"I found your dog," the giant said. "He likes me."

"Ryan, this here is Roy Web. He'd rather you didn't break into the crypt yard at night."

"I was trying to find Steve!" I yelled.

"No need," Roy said, petting the tiny dog. "I got 'im right here."

I walked up for a closer look at Roy and Steve. Roy had a kind face and sad, watery eyes. I had to look way up to see him, so he must have been pushing seven feet tall. I'd seen him around once in awhile, but hardly ever really. He stayed to himself, always had.

Steve was a piece of work. He looked like a little bear cub, only he was about half the size of a whole Subway sandwich. I'm not making that up. This was an extremely small dog. He had one tooth in his head and it was caught on the outside of his lower lip like a fang. Also his tongue was sticking out. Apparently you need front teeth in order to keep your tongue in. Steve was so ugly he was cute. If I had to guess I'd say he was about 2000 years old.

"Steve, you are the coolest looking dog I've ever seen," I said. "Also a troublemaker."

"I agree on both counts," Roy said.

I looked around the crypt yard and thought it was getting a little weird the three of us standing there at night talking about a dog named Steve.

"So listen," I said. "We won't come out here anymore. We were really just looking for Fitz's dog. Sorry about that."

"No problem," Roy said.

He turned and walked away, taking Steve with him. Roy Web had a lumbering walk, like a dinosaur.

Fitz waved me forward and we both followed the cemetery caretaker, who it seemed had taken a liking to Fitz's dog. I sure wasn't going to ask for it back.

When we got out of the crypt yard and the door was locked again, Fitz said something that really surprised me.

"Roy?"

"Yeah?"

"I think my house is haunted. For real."

Roy sat down heavily on one of two metal benches outside the crypt yard door. The metal sagged under his frame. Fitz and I sat on the other bench.

"You really think it's haunted, or you just saying that to mess with ol'

Roy?"

"No I'm serious. I think my house is haunted. It's right over there."

That seemed to interest Roy. His thick eyebrow went up and he stopped petting Steve.

"Could be."

I got the feeling that Fitz trusted Roy because Roy worked with people who were not alive anymore. It was Roy's job to take care of the cemetery, so I guess it sort of added up. If anyone knew about ghosts it would be Roy Web, who buries dead people.

"This here's a town full of secrets, old ones," Roy said. "I recon you've already stumbled onto a few of 'em."

My notoriety as a finder of secrets in the area was fairly well documented. Even Roy Web knew about it.

"So what would you do?" Fitz asked. "If you were me?"

He was hanging on Roy's every

word, but I didn't trust the giant sitting next to us. The guy was the size of a building. He dug holes and put people in them. His hand was bigger than Steve was.

Roy sucked in a boundless gulp of air and exhaled. He looked tired.

"All you gotta do is figure out what a phantom is trying to tell you. After that they'll leave you alone."

"Phantom?" I said. "Why do you call it a phantom?"

"Cause that's what they is. Phantoms."

The way Roy said it rattled me – *Cause that's what they is. Phantoms* – like he really did know what he was talking about.

Roy held Steve up to his face and gave him a good scratch under his tiny chin. Then he handed the dog to Fitz and stood up. He reached out towards a tree standing next to him and picked up a shovel that had been leaning there in the darkness. I was glad it wasn't an ax, but still. Now we were staring up at a giant with a weapon.

"Don't come around here no more," Roy said, his voice a straight line of emotionless track. "Nothing good can come of it."

Fitz stood abruptly as Roy turned to go. "What if I find out what the phantom is trying to tell me. Can I come back and ask you what you think?"

Roy stopped and jabbed the shovel into the dirt a few times. It made a sound that only a shovel against the earth can make. It was not a sound I was particularly interested in hearing at that moment.

Roy looked at us, and I saw in the dimness of the night that the whites of his eyes were yellow and soft. He breathed deeply once more.

"Don't come in here at night. And

don't show up at all unless you really need to. This ain't no place for kids."

"Got it," Fitz said as he started backing away towards his house. "No problem. We'll come back if we discover something. Thanks, Roy."

Roy Web didn't say anything else. His strides were so long the darkness enveloped him in seconds and he was gone.

"So that was weird," I said.

"Yeah. Very," Fitz agreed.

Steve barked like he missed Roy already and we started walking away. Fitz looked at his watch.

"It's 10:30," he said. "I hope Sarah is okay."

"Me too," I agreed.

"I'm still not going in my house until later."

I nodded as we walked in the darkness.

"That makes two of us."

The first sign

When we got to Fitz's house, everything was dark inside. All the lights were off and there was no sign of Sarah. We called out for her but she didn't answer.

"Grab that leash, will ya?" Fitz asked me. It was hanging next to the back door like a noose made for hanging someone.

"Seriously?" I asked.

I checked my phone, nothing new from Sarah. I texted her again.

We're outside at Fitz's house. Where are you??

There was no way Fitz was getting any closer to his house, so I inched my way towards the leash as quietly as I could. When I reached out for it, I half expected the door to open, where a skeleton hand would reach out and grab me, dragging me inside.

"You hear that?" Fitz asked.

I got the leash and ran back.

"Nope," I answered. The only thing I could hear was my heart pounding against my chest.

Fitz shook his head and took a step away from the house. "It's nothing, forget about it."

I was about to ask him what he thought he'd heard when my phone buzzed in my pocket. I checked it while Fitz put the leash on Steve and set him on the ground.

What took you knuckleheads so long? Get to my house. You gotta see this.

"Looks like Sarah has left the scene of the crime," I said. "Come on, she'd got something to show us."

"Anything to get away from this place."

We walked up Main Street with its streetlights spaced out by fifty feet or so. Not even eleven o'clock and the town was dead as a door nail. You'd think this would be peaceful, a small town at night with all its inhabitants snug in bed. But it wasn't. The quieter Skeleton Creek got the scarier it was. Like everyone had vanished or died and we were all alone in the world. Now that's scary.

Sarah's house had a set of stairs that led underground on the side of the house. There was a door at the bottom that she often left unlocked for me. Sarah had recently moved all of her stuff down there, where her parents let her set up shop and pretty much take over the basement.

I knocked and entered simultaneously.

"You guys are not going to believe this," Sarah said.

It was very Sarah like to ignore everything else in the universe when she'd recorded something cool.

"We're fine, thanks for asking," I joked. "Just a little encounter with a seven foot tall grave digger and getting trapped in a crypt yard. Really, it's been fairly boring."

"He's a little sensitive," Fitz said. "We're all in one piece."

The wheels were spinning in Sarah's head. "I'd like to get this seven-footer on tape. Do you think he'd go for it?"

I moved closer to one of her monitors and stared at the screen. "Let's focus on one thing at a time. Looks like you got a camera in there."

"Oh I did better than that," Sarah said. She zipped around me, bumping me in the shoulder as she sat down at mission control. There were so many monitors and computers and cameras on the desk in front of her, I couldn't tell what was connected where.

"How do you work like this?" Fitz asked.

"Is there another way?" Sarah asked seriously. She really didn't think there was any other way to set up shop then the way she'd always done it. "I know where everything is, and it's all getting backed up. It's perfect."

Fitz didn't try to argue. Instead he bent down and let Steve off his leash.

"Glad you found your dog, let's get down to business," Sarah said.

I could tell by the looks of the monitors that she had placed a camera in a room.

"I got there in time to put a camera in place, so we can see what's going on," she began. "Oh, and I put a brand new microphone in there. If this ghost talks, we'll hear it."

"It's a phantom," Fitz said, staring at the images of his mother's room on the

SCREENS.

"YEAH," I SAID. "IT'S A PHANTOM."

"YOU TWO ARE WEIRD," SARAH SAID, TURNING TO HER KEYBOARD. "FINE, PHANTOM. WHATEVER IT IS, YOU WERE RIGHT, FITZ."

"I WAS?"

SHE TYPED OUT A FEW MORE KEY STROKES AND ONE OF THE MONITORS SWITCHED TO AN EARLIER TIME.

"YEAH. YOU'RE HOUSE IS DEFINITELY HAUNTED."

WHAT WE SAW ON THE MONITOR HAS TO BE SEEN TO BE BELIEVED. SOMETIMES I STILL DON'T BELIEVE IT. BUT THERE IT WAS, RIGHT IN FRONT OF US.

SOMETHING HAPPENED.

SARAH MOVED ALL THE VIDEOS WE THINK ARE IMPORTANT TO HER SERVER SO WE CAN ACCESS THEM ONLINE, BUT YOU'LL NEED A PASSWORD.

GO.

GO RIGHT NOW!

DON'T TURN ANOTHER PAGE UNTIL YOU

SEE WHAT SARAH RECORDED IN FITZ'S HOUSE. DON'T BE TEMPTED TO READ FURTHER IN MY JOURNAL UNTIL YOU WATCH THIS VIDEO! IT'S THE VERY START OF SOMETHING INCREDIBLE.

SARAHFINCHER.COM

Password:

TELLTALEHEART

Enter the phantom room

If you dare.

CHANDELIER

WE WATCHED IT THREE TIMES BEFORE SARAH TURNED ON THE AUDIO. IT WAS SCARY ENOUGH IN SILENCE, BUT WITH THE AUDIO ON IT WAS ENOUGH TO SEND ME RUNNING FROM THE ROOM; SOMETHING I WOULD HAVE DONE IF IT HADN'T LED OUT INTO THE NIGHT. NO ONE OUT THERE WAS GOING TO HELP ME.

THE ROOM HAD LOOKED SO STILL AND LIFELESS, SO EMPTY. NOTHING WAS HAPPENING, NOTHING WAS GOING TO HAPPEN. AND THEN SOMETHING DID.

AS YOU'VE ALREADY SEEN BECAUSE YOU DID NOT SKIP WATCHING THAT VIDEO (!), THE CHANDELIER STARTS TO MOVE BACK AND FORTH, EVER SO SLOWLY, AS IF SOMEONE HAS TAKEN IT IN THEIR HAND AND PULLED ON IT. THEN IT MOVED A LOT MORE. IT SWAYED AND JERKED AND SPUN.

"THERE'S NO WAY THAT WAS THE WIND," SARAH SAID AFTER WE WATCHED IT THE FIRST TIME. "FOR STARTERS THERE'S NO BREEZE IN THERE. THE WINDOWS ARE CLOSED AND sealed off by the curtain."

"Something moved the chandelier, but what?" I asked. "There has to be an explanation."

That was when Sarah turned on the audio and we listened to the empty room. At first there was nothing, but then the sound of the glass pendants on the chandelier rang like a wind chime on a summer breeze. I used to like the sound of wind chimes. Now I'll hate that sound for the rest of my life. Sad face.

"What's that other sound?" I asked Sarah. "It's behind the sound of the chandelier."

When the chandelier stopped moving, a voice remained. It was a harsh whisper that sounded like it belonged to a woman.

"See what I mean? She's saying Sid, right?" Fitz asked. "Like the name Sid I mean?"

"Yeah, I think that's it," Sarah said.

"Along with a lot of other sounds that belong in a horror movie."

It was true. There were noises coming out of that room that were hard to figure out. There were echoing clangs, as if metal tools had been thrown down a long hallway. There were distant, unintelligible voices.
An hour later, after talking through our options, we decided not to tell anyone. We arrived at this decision for three reasons:

1) We were the Crossbones. The three of us, together. If we'd thought this wouldn't mean uncovering more haunting secrets about Skeleton Creek, we were wrong. This was our job now, no one else's.

2) We'd been down this road before with adults. They never believed us, never understood. And they always got

IN THE WAY OF FIGURING THINGS OUT.

3) MOST IMPORTANTLY, FITZ WAS A MINOR LIVING ALONE. HE WAS WORRIED THAT IF WE TOLD ANYONE, THEY MIGHT MAKE HIM GO LIVE WITH HIS UNCLE IN BAKER CITY, AND THAT WAS SOMETHING FITZ REALLY DID NOT WANT TO DO. AS LONG AS FITZ'S DAD WAS MISSING, WE HAD TO KEEP A LID ON IT FOR FITZ'S SAKE.

"LET'S FILM AGAIN TOMORROW NIGHT, SEE IF IT'S THE SAME," SARAH SUGGESTED. "WHAT'S THE WORST THAT CAN HAPPEN?"

"WE COULD GET SUCKED INTO THE EVIL VORTEX OF A PHANTOM ROOM!" I SAID.

SARAH ROLLED HER EYES.

"WE'RE NOT IN THE HOUSE WHEN THESE THINGS HAPPEN. NO ONE IS GETTING SUCKED INTO AN EVIL VORTEX."

FITZ LOOKED BACK AND FORTH AT BOTH OF US. "THIS IS HAPPENING? I MEAN, IT'S REAL?"

SARAH AND I HAD ENDURED A LOT MORE

of this type of thing than Fitz had. He hadn't gone down the long dark road searching for Old Joe Bush. He hadn't been a part of so many things we'd already been through. As I watched him staring at us with that moon shaped face of his, I felt sorry for him.

"Look, Fitz, there has to be an explanation for this. And we're going to figure out what it is together."

Fitz picked up Steve and petted him on the head. "Little dude, we are not staying at the house tonight."

"You can stay with me, no problem," I said.

We agreed to call it a night and return to Fitz's house in the morning, when it was light and we were as far away from 10:07PM as we could get.

The door

Fitz slept on the floor and we made a little bed out of old sweatshirts for Steve. You wouldn't think a dog that tiny could snore so loud, but Steve kept me up half the night. I lay there, staring at the ceiling, thinking of the dredge and Sarah and Old Joe Bush. There was something about that whole thread of my life that still felt unfinished. Something told me I'd have to face a ghost in a dredge again before the Crossbones were through.

But for now we had a different problem. Skeleton Creek was full of secrets and lies. The situation at Fitz's house was nothing new, but I was sure there was some kind of history there. Something from the past was causing this to happen, because that's always the way it was in Skeleton Creek. The past came back to haunt us.

The next morning at breakfast I practically fell asleep in my pancakes. "Sam Fitzsimmons, you can really eat," my mom said as she slid the fifth pancake onto his plate.

"Yes ma'am, trying to beef up for football next year."

"I think it's working," I said, staring at Fitz's wide frame. "You're like a bigfoot."

"Stop teasing him, Ryan," my mom said. "You could use a few pounds yourself."

She slid another pancake on my plate even though I hadn't finished my first one.

"How's your dad doing?" my mom asked Fitz as she turned for the griddle in the kitchen. "Haven't seen him around lately."

Fitz looked at me pleadingly, like he'd blown their cover and was already headed to his uncle's house.

"Uhhh, actually he's been out in the woods a lot," Fitz stammered. He scratched his nappy head. "That wind storm in the spring dropped some big trees."

There was a long pause and then my mom turned around.

"Trees?"

Fitz was falling apart.

"Oh, yeah. You know, trees. They fell down. In the storm."

I jumped in before Fitz could do any more damage: "He means firewood, Mom. There's firewood up there."

My mom perked up.

"Well in that case tell your dad if he's selling, we're buying."

She poured more pancake batter and the griddle sizzled then she yelled up the stairs.

"Paul!"

My mom shook her head like she had been waiting on my dad her entire life. I kicked Fitz in the shin under the table and he looked up as he poured syrup. The last thing I wanted was a two parent inquisition about Fitz and his living arrangements. Fitz had almost blown it already. We had to get out of there. I leaned down and handed my last pancake to Steve, who bit into it with his one tooth and began shaking his head like he had a live fish in his mouth.

"We gotta run out and do some stuff before work at the fly shop," I said. "Tell dad we'll be there on time, for sure."

"But I've got all these pancakes," she pleaded. "Here, take some with you."

She put two pancakes each between some napkins and shoved them in our hands.

"Looks like Steve's good to go," she said, staring down at the tiny dog. Steve stared up happily with the pancake hanging out of his mouth. It was three times as big as his head.

It was summer, so the town had a light buzz of tourist activity as Fitz and I high tailed it to Sarah's house. This was

A new phenomenon, caused entirely by the ghost hunting work Sarah and I had done in the past. For better or worse, we'd brought a little bit of fame and fortune to Skeleton Creek.

A couple of cute girls stopped us on the sidewalk and went crazy for Steve.

"Lucky dog," I whispered to Fitz.

"What's his name?" one of the girls asked. She was still down on one knee, smiling at the dog. She didn't even look up.

"Steve," Fitz said.

Now both girls looked up.

"Steve?"

"Sure. Steve," Fitz repeated.

The girls laughed and shook their heads and moved on. I could hear one of them saying *Who names a dog Steve? That's just weird.*

We stopped in to see Sarah, who had overslept. She stood on the front

STEPS OF HER HOUSE WITH A BOWL OF CEREAL AND A BLEARY LOOK IN HER EYES. I COULD TELL SHE'D BEEN UP LATE, SCOURING THROUGH THAT VIDEO, TRYING TO FIND MORE CLUES. TURNED OUT SHE'D FOUND NOTHING MORE, BUT SHE WAS EXCITED TO TRY AGAIN AT 10:07PM THAT NIGHT.

WHEN WE GOT TO FITZ'S HOUSE WE BOTH LOOKED OUT TOWARDS THE CEMETERY. IT'S NOT OFTEN A GRAVEYARD LOOKS MORE INVITING THAN A HOUSE, BUT IN THIS CASE, I THINK WE BOTH THOUGHT ABOUT WHICH WAY TO GO. IT WAS A BRIGHT SUNNY MORNING, AND STILL THE HOUSE FELT LIKE IT WAS ENVELOPED IN DARKNESS.

"MAYBE I'LL JUST WEAR THE CLOTHES I ALREADY HAVE ON," FITZ SAID.

"NO WAY," I ARGUED. "A MAN'S GOTTA CHANGE SOCKS AND UNDERWEAR AT LEAST ONCE A DAY. TWICE IF THE OPTION PRESENTS ITSELF."

I OPENED THE DOOR FOR HIM AND WENT INSIDE. ONCE WE WERE IN THERE, FITZ SET

Steve down and Steve ran right to the stairs and hopped them one at a time until he was gone from sight.

"Perfect," Fitz said. "He just went in my mom's old room."

"The phantom room?" I stammered.

"Yup."

"I guess he does have that one tooth to protect himself."

"And he just ate a whole pancake, so he's got the fuel for some sweet ninja moves."

We both laughed nervously, glad to get our minds off of the potentially haunted house we were standing in.

While Fitz changed clothes I stared up at the phantom room. The stairs reminded me of the one's at the dredge, old and wooden. I had climbed up those stairs, but I hadn't climbed down. I'd fallen and nearly died. I can't tell you why I found myself walking up those stairs, heading towards Fitz's moms room,

BUT I DID. MY LEGS FELT LIKE THEY WERE MADE OF HEAVY IRON, BUT I KEPT GOING UNTIL I REACHED THE LANDING AT THE TOP. STEVE CAME RUNNING OUT OF THE DOOR, PASSED ME, AND TORE DOWN THE STEPS. HE WAS FAST FOR SUCH A LITTLE GUY, AND I WAS REALLY BUMMED THAT NOW I WAS STANDING ALONE IN FRONT OF THE PHANTOM ROOM. I LOOKED INSIDE, BUT DIDN'T GO IN.

"IS THERE A GHOST IN THIS ROOM?" I ASKED OUT LOUD.

A FEW SECONDS PASSED AND I COULD HEAR MYSELF BREATHING. THEN SOMETHING UNEXPECTED HAPPENED.

THE DOOR TO THE ROOM SLAMMED SHUT.

MAYBE THE WINDOW WAS OPEN AFTER ALL IN THERE AND A GUST HAD BLOWN THROUGH, BUT I WOULD NEVER KNOW BECAUSE I WAS ALL THE WAY DOWN THOSE STAIRS THREE AT A TIME IN ABOUT ONE SECOND FLAT. I EVEN FELL DOWN AT THE BOTTOM, SLIDING ACROSS THE WOOD FLOOR.

"You okay out there?" Fitz yelled from his first floor room. "Sounds like you're having a dance party."

"Nope, no dance party here," I said. "Just playing with Steve."

I didn't tell Fitz about the door while we were working all day at my dad's fly shop.

I didn't mention it afterwards, when we went back to my house and played video games.

Even when we met up with Sarah later that night and the sun had gone down, I didn't mention it.

I guess I didn't want to scare him any more than he already was.

The pictures

That night, Sarah pulled a fast one on us. She had it in her head that being at Fitz's house rather than at hers watching the video feed was the only way to be

SURE WE WERE GETTING EVERYTHING.

"FROM HERE I CAN HARDWIRE INTO THE CAMERA IN THE ROOM," SHE SAID. "IF WE DO IT REMOTE FROM MY HOUSE, WE LOSE SOME QUALITY. AND THERE ARE SECURITY ISSUES."

"WHAT KIND OF SECURITY ISSUES?" FITZ ASKED, WAVING STEVE IN FRONT OF HIM WITHOUT THINKING. HE'D TAKEN TO HOLDING THE DOG MOST OF THE TIME, AND SOMETIMES HE FORGOT STEVE WAS IN HIS HAND.

"ARE YOU GOING TO HOLD THAT DOG ALL THE TIME NOW?" SARAH ASKED. "IT'S GETTING A LITTLE BIZARRE."

"IF I PUT HIM DOWN HE'LL MAKE A RUN FOR THE CEMETERY. AND I GET TIRED OF KEEPING HIM ON A LEASH ALL THE TIME."

"ANYWAY," SARAH SAID. "YES, SECURITY ISSUES. IT'S NOT DIFFICULT TO TAP INTO A WIFI FEED, AND I DON'T THINK WE WANT ANYONE KNOWING ABOUT THIS. NOT YET ANYWAY."

I LOOKED AT FITZ AND HE LOOKED AT ME. WE WERE BOTH THINKING THE SAME THING.

"This is Skeleton Creek," I said. "People around here barely have dial up, let alone hardcore hacking skills."

Sarah shrugged. "Can't be too careful."

I preferred the idea of being at least several blocks away at 10:07PM, but as we arrived at 10:05PM there we were, standing right outside of Fitz's house. A cord ran into the back door and up the stairs, where it was attached to a camera.

"I feel like we're standing in the blast zone of a bomb about to go off," Fitz said. "And we have no cover."

"Agree," I said.

"Don't worry so much you guys, we're fine," Sarah said as she clicked some commands onto her keyboard. "Here, put these on."

She had rigged up three sets of headphones so we could all listen in on the room while we watched. I put mine on and heard soft static fill my ears.

We all sat down at a picnic table on Fitz's back porch, staring into Sarah's laptop. The screen was filled with a room. There were framed pictures and a bookshelf along one wall, divided by long curtains covering a window. The headboard for the bed had been fashioned out of two antique doors.

"Nice headboard," I said.

"Yeah, my mom was into junkin'," Fitz said. "She loved garage sales and antique stores. It was sort of her thing to repurpose old stuff."

"That's cool," Sarah said. "Did you know some people are literally afraid of antique furniture? It's like a phobia."

"That is the strangest phobia I've ever heard of," I said, although I'd heard of some very odd ones.

Sarah disagreed: "Not really. What they're afraid of is who owned it. So like maybe there's a dresser built in 1759.

Think of all the places that dresser has been, all the things it's held, the people who owned it. Maybe somewhere along the line there were bad things in those drawers."

"You mean like underwear?" Fitz said.

I laughed nervously. "Or socks?"

Sarah glared at us. "Or maybe a severed hand?"

Thinking about all of this, I suddenly decided I did not like antique furniture.

"It's time," Sarah said.

I looked at my phone and saw that it was indeed time. 10:07PM.

Fitz peeled off his headphones. "I'm just going to right stand over here, next to the cemetery. Where it's safe."

I'm not sure Sarah even heard Fitz say those words. She was locked in on the screen, watching and listening carefully. She was very determined and

FOCUSED WHEN SHE WANTED TO BE.

TEN MINUTES LATER NOTHING HAD HAPPENED.

ANOTHER TEN MINUTES PASSED AND FITZ CAME BACK, CALMER, AND PUT HIS HEADPHONES BACK ON.

"MAYBE IT KNOWS WE'RE OUT HERE, FILMING IT," HE SAID. "MAYBE IT'S NOT GOING TO HAPPEN."

HE LEANED IN VERY CLOSE, HIS FACE ALMOST TOUCHING THE SCREEN, AND THAT'S WHEN IT DID HAPPENED.

YOU NEED TO SEE THIS. YOU REALLY DO. IT'S SO MUCH MORE REVEALING IF YOU'RE ABLE TO LOOK YOURSELF.

GO WATCH THE VIDEO WE SHOT THAT NIGHT. GO RIGHT NOW!

I'LL WAIT HERE AND TRY NOT TO SCREAM.

SARAHFINCHER.COM

PASSWORD:

PROSPERO

ENTER THE PHANTOM ROOM

IF YOU DARE.

INTO THE ROOM

SO NOW YOU'VE SEEN WHAT WE SAW. IT'S OUR SECRET, AND I'VE SHARED IT WITH YOU. YOU'VE HEARD THE SAME THING WE DID: THAT WHISPERING VOICE SAYING THE SAME THING OVER AND OVER. SID! SID! SID! AND YOU SAW WHAT WE SAW.

FIRST A PICTURE MOVED ON THE WALL, AS IF IT WAS NO LONGER HELD IN ONE PLACE BY A NAIL. THEN ANOTHER PICTURE. IT WAS AS IF THEY WERE NO LONGER ATTACHED, SLIDING SILENTLY TO NEW POSITIONS.

AND THEN, AS IF WE'D JUST HAD AN EARTHQUAKE IN SKELETON CREEK, THEY FELL TO THE FLOOR.

NOT ALL OF THEM, JUST FOUR. ONLY FOUR PICTURES FELL, AND IT WAS SARAH WHO ASKED WHAT WE WERE ALL WONDERING.

"I THINK IT'S TRYING TO TELL US SOMETHING," SHE SAID. "THE PHANTOM. IT'S TALKING TO US."

"YEAH BUT WE DON'T KNOW WHAT SID MEANS," I REMINDED HER. WE'D KNOWN ABOUT the whispering already.

"No, I mean the pictures."

Sarah was suggesting that there was something important about those particular pictures, the ones that had fallen.

"Wait, you're not saying what I think you're saying," I said, because I already knew what Sarah was thinking.

"Someone needs to go in there and get those pictures," she said.

"Why did I know she was going to say that?" Fitz joked.

We all sat there, staring at the still room. Everything had gone quiet. No audio, no movement, just a normal everyday room.

We took off our headphones and sat at the table.

"I'll do it," Fitz said, surprising both me and Sarah.

Steve barked, scaring the daylights out of me.

"Are you sure about this?" Sarah asked. "Maybe we should all go."

"No, you stay here and watch the video feed," I said, standing up from the picnic table. "I'll go with Fitz. We'll do it together."

Fitz stood up too, taking a big breath and holding the dog out to Sarah.

"Hold Steve, we're going in."

I'm not gonna lie, I did not want to go into the house let alone the phantom room. Who would? But Fitz was my buddy and there was no way I was letting him go it alone.

"Let's do this," I said, rubbing my hands together like an idiot. My palms were clammy, my legs were shaking, and my brain was in total panic mode. But I walked to the door and pushed it open. Fitz and I moved slowly, like a couple of cat burglars, turning on lights as we went. When we reached the bottom of the stairs, Fitz put his arm in front of my chest like he was protecting me from a car crash.

"Let me do this alone," he said. "I haven't been in there for awhile. I need to do this."

I tried to imagine what it would be like if I was going up to my mom's room and she'd been dead a long time. It would be hard, for sure.

"Hey I just thought of something," I said when Fitz was on the third step. "Maybe it's your mom. Maybe she's trying to tell you something."

Fitz looked back at me, his big frame like the shadow of a yeti staring down at me.

"I've been thinking the same thing."

I'm not sure if it was because I couldn't let my friend go up there alone or because I didn't want to be left on the first floor by myself, but I followed behind Fitz. He looked back and didn't protest, so I kept going.

When we arrived at the door to his mom's room, he pushed it gently open. Inside it looked perfectly calm and peaceful. A small light was on in the corner, a light Sarah had turned on when she was setting up her camera. The moment Fitz stepped into the room, the light went out.

And not just that light.

All the lights in the house went out.

To my credit I didn't freak out entirely, although I did make a small scream sound that was eaten up by the darkness in nothing flat. Fitz took out his phone and shone the light into the room. He seemed remarkably calm.

"Good call," I said, taking my own phone out and shining even more light into the space.

Shadows were cast everywhere, making the corners of the room dark with things that might jump out at us. I couldn't look at the bed, because it made me wonder what was under the bed.

Fitz knelt down and picked up the pictures. When he did, the voice returned. Sid. Sid. Sid.

"Come on, Fitz! Let's get out of here," I said.

"It's my mom," Fitz said. "It totally is."

I grabbed Fitz by the shirt sleeve and pulled him towards the door. He followed reluctantly, and as soon as we were in the hallway, the door to the room slammed shut on its own.

That was enough to send me flying down the stairs at triple speed. When I got to the bottom, Fitz was close behind and he nearly knocked me over. We scrambled for the back door.

Breathing fresh, non-haunted air was the best feeling in the world at that moment. We'd entered a phantom room and lived to tell about it. I have to admit, it was kind of cool.

The four pictures

We sat at the picnic table as the bugs danced against the porch light making tiny pinging sounds. The air had begun to cool, a classic summer night in the mountains bearing down on us. I loved this about Skeleton Creek: a summer day could hover close to 100, but the nights were always cool, like a glass of cold water.

The moon was still full and the tombstones from the cemetery cast soft shadows into the night. We huddled close together and set the four pictures out in a row.

There was something I'd been wanting to ask Fitz, but I'd been to chicken. Now, with these pictures in front of us, I felt like it was time.

"Fitz, I need to ask you something." Fitz looked at me. So did Steve.

"You sent me a letter once and in it you said you're mom had taken off before you were three. Why'd you tell me that if she's dead?"

Fitz's face darkened and he couldn't hold my stare.

"I guess I wasn't ready to tell you the truth is all."

I nodded a couple of times and Sarah did, too.

"Hey, it's okay," she said. "I'm sorry she's gone. I mean like really gone."

"It's more than that," he said. Fitz scratched under Steve's chin and stared at the dogs face as he spoke. "They took my mom away."

"Who? Who took your mom?" I asked.

Fitz gulped a big breath of air.

"It took me a long time to get my dad to tell me the truth. I guess she was never the same after I was born. She was...I don't know, loony I guess. They put her in a hospital. As far as I know she never got out. She died in there."

"Whoa," Sarah said. "I mean, sorry. Sorry, Fitz."

"Yeah well, everyone's got something, right?" he said, shrugging it off.

"Yeah but that's a pretty big something," I said, standing up and patting him on the shoulder. "It's not your fault, obviously. Stuff just happens."

Sarah nodded and fiddled with the keys on her laptop.

"Are you sure she's, you know, gone?"

Fitz sat staring at the pictures. "Yeah, she's dead. That much is for sure."

It was hard to know what to do next. Things had gotten even heavier than I thought possible, and it seemed like a good time to call it a night.

"I sometimes think she's trying to talk to me," Fitz said. "Trying to tell me something important. I think it's her you guys. It's my mom. There's some unfinished business going on here."

"That sounds like a Crossbones job to me," Sarah said, and it was just the right thing at the right time. "We're in this together, the three of us. If Fitz's mom is trying to tell us something, then we have to figure out what it is."

I looked at Fitz. No way I was going to be the next vote. It had to be him.

"Agreed," he said. Steve barked. "And Steve agrees, too."

I smiled, happy that I had two people who I could totally trust, my best friends.

"Agreed," I said.

We carefully examined each of the four pictures, looking for clues to what the phantom was trying to tell us.

"What is she trying to say?" Sarah mused, barely above a whisper.

"I asked my dad about all these

pictures. This one was taken in front of the Eifel Tower," Fitz said. The picture was a young woman, pretty and full of life, standing in front of the Tower. "She's on a college trip to Paris, before she ever met my dad and long before I was born."

"She was gorgeous," Sarah said. She was the only Crossbones member who could say something like that and get away with it.

Fitz smiled sadly. "Thanks, Sarah. She was a pretty lady, for sure."

"What about this one?" I asked, pointing to the second picture. I wasn't sure if Fitz's mom was in it.

"She's at Deer Valley Lodge, in Montana. My mom grew up in Hamilton, this small Montana town. They vacationed at this lodge. That's her, right there."

A bunch of cute little kids were sitting on a long porch step, all of them summer tan and mugging for the camera. The kid Fitz pointed to had another kids arm in her hand like it was a turkey leg. She was acting like she was about to bite into it.

"She was a goofy kid, or so I'm told," Fitz said.

"Then she would have fit right in with our little nerd herd," I said encouragingly.

"Maybe she would have even helped us," Sarah said.

There was a pause and Steve barked. Fitz set the dog down and held onto the leash.

"Maybe she is trying to help us," Sarah concluded. "Let's keep going. Where was this one taken?"

Fitz looked at the picture, where his mom was holding up a cup of coffee in front her. She had a mischievous look on her face, like she was about to trip the waitress as she walked by.

"That's Sony's Café, over in Portland," Fitz said. "It's where my mom and dad met."

I couldn't imagine Fitz's dad anywhere but in the woods and I said so.

"There's a lot about my dad that might surprise you. He got really tired of Skeleton Creek when he finished high school and bolted for the city. Ended up working as a short order cook at Sony's. I think he took this picture."

"She must have really loved your dad to follow him all the way up here," Sarah said.

Fitz shrugged. "I guess so."

Then he went on: "The last picture is at Nordstrom's in Seattle. That's me in there."

Fitz was referring to his mom's big round stomach, because in the picture she was pregnant. She was holding up a huge dress made for someone five times her size, pointing to it like this one will fit!

"I like your mom," I said. "She was cool."

"How do you know it's at a Nordstrom? She could be shopping anywhere," Sarah asked.

"I opened the frame a long time ago and looked at the back of the photo. She wrote the date and the location on it."

"Did she write on the others?" Sarah asked, already picking up one of them hoping to find a clue.

"Already checked," Fitz said. "She didn't leave any other notes I could find."

We all stared at the pictures. I wondered if we were trying to find something that wasn't there, but it couldn't hurt to lay out what we had. So I put forth a theory that felt right.

"So we know there are four places these pictures were taken: the Eifel Tower, Sony's Café, Nordstrom's, and

Deer Valley Lodge. Maybe that means something, like we're supposed to decode those locations somehow."

"That's not much to go on," Sarah said. "But if there's some message here, I think you're right. It has to do with the locations. That's the common thread: four pictures, four places."

Fitz stared up at the back of the house and breathed the cool night air.

"There's something I haven't told you guys yet," Fitz said. "I thought you'd think I was crazy."

Sarah moved closer to Fitz and gave him that narrow eyed gaze I'd seen so many times before, the one that's impossible to say no to.

"Tell us," she said.

Fitz kicked the dirt at his feet and watched Steve, who was looking longingly towards the cemetery.

"She'll answer me," Fitz said.

Sarah's head moved back on her

neck and her eyes widened. "Wait, you mean your mom? How?"

"The first and only night I stayed here alone, before you guys found me in the cemetery, I went up there during the haunting hour."

Fitz stopped short of saying anything else.

"And?" I asked, on the edge of my seat.

"And I asked some questions. The phantom room answered."

Fitz turned in the direction of my house and pulled Steve along gently, calling for him to follow.

"Wait, how did it answer?" Sarah asked.

Fitz kept walking. He'd had enough for one night. It was different for him, more emotional. It wasn't my mom or Sarah's mom in the phantom room. It was Fitz's.

"Let him go," I said. "We'll find out

soon enough. He needs a break."

Sarah nodded but she wasn't happy about the turn of events. I got up to follow Fitz into the darkness, but Sarah called us both back.

"You guys!" Sarah said with some amazement in her voice. "It's back on."

Fitz and I circled back and stood staring at the monitor on Sarah's laptop.

The light had turned back on in the phantom room while we were busy looking at pictures.

"Let's do this again tomorrow night," Fitz said. "I'll show you how the room answers me."

Sarah smiled and closed her laptop, and then she said what I was thinking.

"Now we're talking."

Snoring

I had a fitful night of tossing and turning while I listened to Steve snore like a chainsaw. Man, that little dog could really make some noise. About midnight Fitz started snoring too, and it was like a buzz saw symphony I couldn't possibly sleep through.

There was a quiet knock at my door and it opened eerily.

My dad peeked through the opening and looked at the two bodies on the floor: one was Fitz, the other was Steve.

"Wow," he whispered.

"Tell me about it," I whispered back.

He came in and stood next to my bed, arms crossed at his chest as he looked at the two of them and shook his head.

"Please tell me this is a temporary arrangement," he said quietly.

"Oh it's temporary," I said. "Just until Fitz's—"

Whoa! I nearly spilled the beans about Fitz's dad having gone missing.

Close call.

"Until Fitz's what?" my dad asked.

"I already told Mom. Fitz's dad is out hauling wood late every night. Fitz would just rather stay here for a little bit."

My dad nodded and looked at me through the darkness. "You're a good friend. How's it going otherwise?"

"Good. Fine," I stammered. "Fly shop is busy and things have really calmed down around here. It's good."

I couldn't believe I was saying things had calmed down when we were chasing down a ghost three blocks away.

Steve stirred and looked up at my dad. He growled.

"Time for me to go," my dad said, and he quickly left the room and shut the door.

"It's okay little buddy, go back to sleep," I said, hoping Steve wouldn't have a barking attack.

He settled down and a few minutes later Steve was snoring again.

I lay there for another hour, wondering about Fitz's mom and how she'd spoken to him.

I finally drifted off to sleep around 1:00AM.

The Phantom Room Speaks

I'm not going to go into all the details of the day that followed or the evening leading up to 10:07PM. The short version is this:

– Got up, ate breakfast, fell asleep at the table.

– Worked at the fly shop all morning with Fitz and my dad.

– Took two businessmen from Portland on an afternoon float, fishing was sub-par.

– Got a lousy tip from said fishermen.

– Ate dinner, fell asleep at the

table. It's a pattern. See previously described snoring roommates.

– Arrived at Fitz's house at 9:45PM, found Sarah already set up and ready to go.

At 10:05PM Fitz picked up Steve with one arm and the four stacked pictures with the other and went inside the house. He seemed less afraid than he was before, now that he was convinced this wasn't just any phantom, it was his mom. It might have also helped that Steve, with his scary snaggletooth, was going in with him.

"Brave dog," Sarah said.

I was focused on other things. "We have no idea what he's going to do up there, do we?"

"Nope," Sarah said.

She dialed Fitz's number on her phone and put it on speaker. She'd outfitted him with a hands free headset so we could stay in touch.

"You there?" Fitz's voice boomed. Sarah turned down the volume on her speaker and told him we were standing by.

"Just about up the stairs. Steve's not liking it up here."

"If you have to come back, we understand," I said.

Sarah's eyes were glued to her monitor.

I looked at the time on my phone screen.

10:07PM.

"Here we go," I said, a little shiver of anticipation in my voice.

We saw the door to the room open, just a shadow of light passing into the room, but Fitz stayed under the camera mount Sarah had set up.

"I see the camera overhead," Fitz said.

His hand entered the screen and he

waved.

"Yeah, you're good," Sarah said. "We see you."

"NO, Steve! Come back here!" Fitz yelled.

It sounded like Steve had bolted for the stairs, which would leave Fitz in there alone.

"It's okay, I have him," Fitz told us in a nervous voice. "He's fine. I had to lay the pictures out in front of me in a row, took two hands."

Sarah looked at me and I could tell she was thinking the same thing I was: *This isn't going very well.*

But she covered for us, she was good at that.

"You're doing great, Fitz. Just stay calm. How does this work?"

Fitz didn't answer at first. It seemed somehow a personal thing with him, or maybe he was afraid it wouldn't work if he tried whatever he'd tried before.

"Open means yes, closed means no," he said.

"Wait, I don't understand?" I said, because I didn't.

But Fitz was done explaining. Now he was going to show us.

We waited, and a few seconds later, Fitz asked a question.

"Do the locations in the four pictures matter?"

Nothing happened for a few seconds, but then something did.

Several things happened, actually. Stuff I still can't believe.

You have to watch the video Sarah posted from that night before you keep reading.

There's no way you can read on without seeing what we saw.

It's going to change the way you feel about this entire situation.

Go watch! I'll be waiting right here when you get back.

SARAHFINCHER.COM

PASSWORD:

SNED

ENTER THE PHANTOM ROOM

IF YOU DARE.

I'VE NEVER BEEN SO FREAKED OUT BY A DOOR IN MY ENTIRE LIFE. YOU SAW WHAT IT DID! IF THE ANSWER WAS YES, THE DOOR OPENED MORE. IF THE ANSWER WAS NO, IT CLOSED MORE.

WE FED QUESTIONS TO FITZ FROM OUTSIDE, FIGURING IT OUT AS WE WENT, AND WHEN WE HAD EVERYTHING JUST RIGHT, THE DOOR SLAMMED SHUT.

AND THEN THERE WAS THAT MESSED UP HAND AT THE END, LIKE SOMEONE TRYING TO ESCAPE THE ROOM. THAT CAME AFTER FITZ WAS GONE AND WHEN HE SAW IT LATER IT REALLY BOTHERED HIM. COULD THAT HAVE BEEN HIS MOM, REACHING OUT FOR FITZ AS HE RAN AWAY?

MAYBE.

THE IMPORTANT THING IS WE FIGURED OUT WHAT THE PICTURES WERE TRYING TO TELL US.

WE KEPT ASKING QUESTIONS UNTIL WE WERE SURE THE LOCATIONS DID MATTER, WE HAD BEEN RIGHT ABOUT THAT. THEN WE ASKED

IF THE FIRST LETTERS MATTERED, AND WE WERE RIGHT ABOUT THAT, TOO.

As Fitz kept re-ordering the pictures, he finally landed on a word.

S for Sony's Cafe.

N for Nordstrom.

E for Eifel Tower.

D for Dear Valley Lodge.

SNED.

That's when the door slammed shut and nearly scared me out of my underwear.

"What the heck does Sned mean?" Sarah was the first to ask.

"Maybe it's like the word we keep hearing in there: Sid," I added. "Maybe the two are related somehow. Sned and Sid." Fitz shook his head in frustration.

"This isn't working at all. Sid? Sned? We're making this up as we go.

It's so confusing!"

I felt bad for Fitz. Here he was hoping for a message from his mom and he was getting frustrated by stuff that made no sense.

"Sorry man, I know this is hard for you," I said. "Should we stop trying?"

"But this is real you guys," Sarah said. "We're the Crossbones. It's our duty to figure out what's happening here. We can't stop."

Fitz set Steve down and picked up a rock. He threw it into the cemetery and we heard it ping against a tombstone. All I could think of was he'd just woken up the dead and probably made at least one of them mad in the process.

"Uh oh," Sarah said.

"What? What is it?" Fitz said, glancing back at her.

"Steve's gone."

Fitz looked around frantically. He'd set Steve down in the dark and the little troublemaker had taken off. And there was only one direction that dog was likely to go.

"He's gone into the cemetery again," I said. "Great."

"No this is good," Sarah said, which both disturbed and surprised me.

What was wrong with her? Fitz was having a crummy time of it and she's glad his dog went missing?

"Come on you guys," she said. "We're going to find Steve. And Roy Web."

I'd forgotten about the very large man with the shiny bald head and the watery eyes.

"She's right," Fitz said. "If anyone can help us, he can. He's the one who got us started on this whole crazy thing to begin with. And Steve loves Roy. If we find Roy, we'll find Steve."

And so we ventured back into the Skeleton Creek cemetery as the clock

EDGED TOWARDS MIDNIGHT.

SNEDIKER

THE SKELETON CREEK CEMETERY IS A LOT BIGGER THAN I THOUGHT IT WAS. IT SEEMED TO GO ON FOR ACRES AND ACRES. THE CRYPT YARD WALLS SAT AT THE FAR EDGE OF THE CEMETERY LIKE A HEART THAT HAD STOPPED BEATING. IT FELT LIKE A MAGNET, HOLDING ALL THE DEAD BODIES IN PLACE SO THEY COULDN'T ESCAPE OUT INTO THE WORLD.

WE CALLED FOR STEVE QUIETLY, TRYING NOT TO DISTURB THE SILENCE, AND WE STAYED TOGETHER. NONE OF US WANTED TO SPLIT UP AS WE SEARCHED UP AND DOWN THE ROWS OF TOMBSTONES. A WARM WIND KICKED UP, SENDING A FEW FALLEN LEAVES SKITTERING IN FRONT OF MY FEET, AND I THOUGHT I HEARD THE SOUND OF A DOG BARKING.

"THIS WAY," FITZ SAID. HE'D HEARD IT, TOO.

FITZ TOOK THE LEAD AND WE PASSED INTO THE FARTHEST CORNER OF THE GROUNDS,

WHERE WE DISCOVERED A SHACK NOT MUCH BIGGER THAN A TOOL SHED. ROY WEB WAS SITTING OUT FRONT AT A TABLE LIT BY A LANTERN.

HE WAS HOLDING STEVE.

"HEY, ROY," FITZ SAID, WAVING AWKWARDLY. "NICE NIGHT OUT. I SEE YOU HAVE MY DOG THERE."

"NOT TOO HOT, NOT TOO COLD," ROY SAID AS HE RAN A HAND ACROSS HIS DARK, BALD HEAD. "JUST THE WAY I LIKE IT."

"STEVE HAS REALLY TAKEN TO YOU," SARAH SAID, EDGING CLOSER.

"HE'S A GOOD DOG," ROY SAID.

I LOOKED TO THE LEFT AND THEN THE RIGHT, AND THEN DID A DOUBLE TAKE TO THE LEFT. ROY HAD DUG A COFFIN SIZE HOLE IN THE GROUND AND LEFT HIS SHOVEL STUCK IN THE DIRT ON ONE END. FOR SOME REASON I COULDN'T HELP WONDERING IF THE SHOVEL WAS AT THE FOOT OR THE HEAD END. THEN I STARTED WONDERING IF THERE WAS A BODY LYING IN THERE.

THEN I SAID SOMETHING STUPID.

"DOING SOME GARDENING, ARE YOU?"

ROY GLANCED OVER AT THE HOLE AND THEN AT ME WITH A RAISED EYEBROW.

"WE'RE GOING TO HAVE TO FIGURE OUT THIS DOG PROBLEM," ROY SAID.

I GUESS HE DIDN'T WANT TO EXPLAIN THE HOLE HE'D DUG AND THAT GOT ME THINKING MAYBE IT HAD BEEN DUG FOR ME. I REALLY NEED TO DO SOMETHING ABOUT MY ACTIVE IMAGINATION.

"YEAH, SORRY ABOUT THAT," SARAH JUMPED IN. "BUT SINCE WE'RE HERE, COULD WE ASK YOU SOMETHING?"

THE WIND SWIRLED THROUGH AGAIN AND THE LANTERN THREW SOFT SHADOWS AND LIGHT ACROSS THE SHED.

ROY DREW A HEAVY SIGH, BUT I COULD TELL HE WASN'T EXACTLY SAD TO SEE US. IT HAD TO BE LONELY OUT THERE, NIGHT AFTER NIGHT.

"HOLD STEVE FOR ME," ROY SAID, AND THEN HE STOOD UP. I'D ALREADY FORGOTTEN

HOW WIDE AND TALL HE WAS. ROY WOULD HAVE MADE A GOOD PRISON GUARD.

FITZ TOOK STEVE AND UNCOILED HIS LEASH FROM A BACK POCKET. HE LEASHED THE DOG AND SET IT ON THE GROUND. STEVE WHIMPERED AS ROY WALKED TOWARDS THE SHED AND I THOUGHT OH GREAT, HE'S GOING IN THERE TO GET THE CHAINSAW OR THE AXE OR A GIANT HAMMER TO FINISH US OFF AND DUMP US IN THE OPEN GRAVE.

"BE RIGHT BACK," HE SAID.

ROY HAD TO BEND DOWN TO ENTER THE DOOR. WHEN HE WAS GONE, WE STARTED ASSESSING THE SITUATION.

"LET'S GET OUT OF HERE," I SAID, SURE THAT MY CROSSBONES PALS WOULD AGREE.

"WHY WOULD WE WANT TO DO THAT?" SARAH SAID.

"BECAUSE HE JUST WENT IN THERE AND HE'S PROBABLY COMING OUT WITH A SHOTGUN OR A SAMURAI SWORD!"

"WALLS ARE PRETTY THIN," ROY SAID FROM INSIDE THE SHED. "AND I DON'T OWN A gun or a sword."

"We haven't even asked him about what happened yet," Fitz said disappointedly.

Roy came out of the shed door head first, using the top of his noggin to push his way out. He had a pitcher in one hand and four small mason jars trapped between his meaty fingers.

"You want to ask me about something," Roy said. "Just ask. I don't mind."

He banged all four glass jars onto the picnic table and removed all his fingers. As he spread the glasses out I thought about the fact that his fingers had just been inside all of them. I hoped he'd washed the dead stuff off his hands as he poured something out of the pitcher.

"Sit down with ol' Roy," he said. "Have some lemonade. Best stuff on earth."

We all eyed each other like are

we doing this? And then I sat down first because I didn't know what else to do.

"You can let him off the leash," Roy said. "He ain't goin' anywhere."

Fitz thought twice about this, but then Roy dug into his shirt pocket and pulled out something small I couldn't see and tossed it at Steve's feet. The dog gobbled it up and I hoped against all hope that he hadn't just fed Fitz's dog something he'd dug up out of the ground earlier in the day.

We all sat down and Fitz let Steve roam around, off the leash.

"So Roy," Sarah said, the boldest by far of the Crossbones. And then she told him all about what we'd seen and what we'd been doing since we'd last seen him.

"We've been trying to get answers from this phantom, just like you said," Fitz jumped in. "And we think we found something it's trying to tell us."

One of Roy's eyebrows went up, crinkling his wide forehead. He sipped at his lemonade and I figured if he was drinking it wasn't poison so I tried some, too. It had a perfect balance of tart and sweet and it was ice cold. I thought to myself: this is really good, but he must have a meat locker in there to keep it so cold. What else has he got frozen in there?

"We think it gave us a word," I said, since I hadn't spoken since we sat down and I was feeling sort of useless. "Sned." This really got Roy's attention and *both* eyebrows went up.

"Well now that is something," he said. "Something indeed."

Sarah was about to explode she was so excited.

"Can you tell us what it means?" she asked.

Roy looked down at the picnic table and dug into his overalls. Out

CAME A KNIFE, WHICH HE OPENED UP AND BEGAN CARVING INTO THE TABLE WITH. IT WAS UNNERVING, TO SAY THE LEAST.

"KARL SNEDIKER," HE SAID. "HE'S THE MAN RUNS THIS HERE CEMETERY. REAL QUIET GUY, NOT AROUND MUCH. EVERYONE WHO KNOWS HIM CALLS HIM SNED."

FITZ HAD A PUZZLED LOOK ON HIS FACE. "WHY WOULD A PHANTOM GIVE US THIS GUY'S NAME?"

ROY TURNED THE KNIFE IN HIS HAND AND STABBED INTO THE TABLE, MAKING US ALL JUMP SEVERAL INCHES OUT OF OUR SEATS. I MIGHT HAVE MADE A SMALL WHIMPERING SOUND.

"KARL SNEDIKER IS MY BOSS," HE SAID. "SNED'S NOT A FRIENDLY KINDA GUY. HE DON'T LIKE KIDS, ANIMALS, OR ANY OTHER UNINVITED GUESTS ON THE GROUNDS. AND HE HATES IT MOST WHEN SOMEONE TRIES TO ENTER THE CRYPT YARD."

"MAYBE HE'S HIDING SOMETHING," SARAH SAID, EVER THE SLEUTH.

Roy shrugged and yanked the knife out of the table. He folded the blade and put the knife back in his overalls. I thought this was a good development.

"Sned is secretive, always has been. He's misunderstood. He gets angry. Better to avoid him if you can. It's why I keep telling you all to stay away. No good can come from snooping around in Karl Snediker's cemetery."

"It's not like he owns it though," Fitz said. "Right?"

Roy shook his head.

"Nope. Town owns it, but Sned runs it. This one and some others. That's why he's not here. He's got other places to watch over."

"But why is a phantom trying to tell us something about him?" I persisted.

"Hard to say," Roy answered. "Sned's been around a long, long time. Maybe he's in cahoots with this phantom of yours. I'll ask him, how about that?"

"Why can't we ask him ourselves?" Sarah asked, and it felt like she was crossing a line.

Roy stood up.

"Did I mention he hates kids? And dogs? Steve wouldn't last five minutes if ol' Sned knew he was running around the graveyard. I'll ask him, I promise. But he's very busy. He don't come around much anymore."

I thought of the other word we'd heard whispered again and again and ventured one more question.

"Does Kark Snediker know a guy named Sid? Maybe they're brothers."

Roy laughed.

"Ol' Sned, he ain't got no brother I ever heard about. But I'll ask him."

We all stood up because it felt like Roy was done talking to us. Steve barked and everyone looked in the direction of the hole Roy had dug.

Steve was staring down into it, growling.

"Come on, Steve," Fitz said. "Come here boy."

Steve ran over and stood next to Roy, but Fitz picked him up. I'm not sure I would have had the guts to do that. Down low at Roy's feet was like looking up at an NBA center that could kick you into next week.

Roy turned around and headed for his door.

"Oh, one more thing," Fitz said as Roy ducked to go inside. "I think this phantom is my mom."

Roy paused but didn't turn around. Then he was gone inside the shack and we were alone with the hole in the ground and the pitcher of lemonade.

"I'm outta here," I said.

We all double timed it out of the cemetery, more suspicious of Roy then we'd been before we arrived.

FISH ON

FITZ AND I GOT A PIECE OF BAD LUCK THE NEXT MORNING WHEN WE SHOWED UP AT THE FLY SHOP: A FAMILY OF FOUR HAD BOOKED A LATE THREE DAY RUN DOWN THE RIVER. 40 MILES OF FISHING WITH TWO PARENTS AND TWO KIDS. THIS MEANT TWO NIGHTS RIVERSIDE, SETTING UP CAMP, FEEDING EVERYONE, AND SPENDING MOST OF OUR DAY ON DIFFERENT BOATS.

UGH.

I CAN'T BEGIN TO TELL YOU HOW LONG THOSE TWO DAYS WERE. NO CELL SERVICE WHATSOEVER, WHICH NORMALLY I WOULD LIKE. BUT NOT WHEN WE'RE CHASING DOWN A PHANTOM!

FITZ LEFT STEVE WITH SARAH AND WE SPENT THE NEXT THREE DAYS UNTANGLING LINE, TEACHING PEOPLE HOW TO CAST, AND ROWING DRIFT BOATS FROM MORNING UNTIL NIGHT. AT LEAST THE FISHING WAS GOOD, AND THE KIDS TOOK TO IT BETTER THAN MOST. IT COULD HAVE BEEN WORSE. THREE DAYS ON

A RIVER IS NEVER FUN WHEN THE FISH AREN'T BITING, ESPECIALLY IF YOU'RE THE GUIDE. YOU GET A LOT OF DUMB QUESTIONS WHEN THAT HAPPENS.

– SHOULD WE TRY SOME DIFFERENT FLIES?

– MAYBE WE SHOULD PUT A WORM ON THAT HOOK?

– I DON'T THINK WE SHOULD CAST OVER THERE ANYMORE, SHOULD WE?

– MAYBE IF WE START EARLIER IN THE MORNING IT WILL GET BETTER?

THE THING ABOUT COMMENTS LIKE THESE, AND THEY ARE UNIVERSAL ON SLOW DAYS, IS THAT THEY PRESUME FITZ AND I HAVE NO IDEA WHAT WE'RE DOING. WE'VE BOTH BEEN FISHING SKELETON CREEK OUR ENTIRE LIVES. WE'VE FLOATED THE RIVER OVER A THOUSAND DAYS BETWEEN US. WE KNOW EXACTLY WHERE TO CAST, WHEN TO CAST, WHAT TO CAST. IF THE FISH AREN'T BITING, IT'S

BECAUSE THEY'RE NOT HUNGRY.

IT WAS ALSO A FULL MOON, SO I KNEW THAT WAS GOING TO MESS THINGS UP. FULL MOONS ARE TERRIBLE FOR FISHING, BECAUSE IT'S LIGHT AT NIGHT. THAT MEANS THE FISH FEED ALL NIGHT LONG AND THEN WHEN OUR BOAT FLOATS BY THEY'RE SLEEPING IN A HAMMOCK SOMEWHERE AT THE BOTTOM OF THE RIVER.

ANYWAY, I DIGRESS.

THE WHOLE POINT IS TO SAY THIS WAS A GIANT BUMMER. IMAGINE YOU'RE ONTO SOMETHING THIS BIG, THIS CRAZY, AND THEN YOU HAVE TO GO OUT INTO THE WILDERNESS WITH NO PHONE FOR THREE DAYS AND PUT EVERYTHING ON HOLD. AND IT GETS WORSE! YOU'RE ON A BOAT WITH PEOPLE YOU DON'T KNOW, SO YOU CAN'T EVEN TALK ABOUT THE AWESOME THING YOU LEFT BEHIND.

IT WAS THE LONGEST THREE DAYS OF MY LIFE, I KID YOU NOT. BUT WE DID EVENTUALLY MAKE IT BACK, AND WHEN WE DID, WE DISCOVERED SOMETHING WE DID NOT

EXPECT.

What Fitz and I didn't know was that Sarah had continued the investigation without us.

She went in the phantom room alone while we were gone. What happened there broke things wide open. It also appears to have made the phantom very angry.

Sarah and the phantom room

"You did what?!"

I think Fitz and I said those three words at the exact same time when Sarah told us what she'd done.

"I went in the phantom room last night," she said for the second time, shrugging as if it was nothing. But I knew Sarah better than anyone, and I could tell it was definitely more than nothing.

"I can't believe you did that without us!" Fitz said.

We'd left Steve with Sarah, and

FITZ PICKED UP THE DOG AND LOOKED IT OVER.

"DON'T WORRY, I TOOK GOOD CARE OF STEVE," SHE SAID.

WE WERE IN SARAH'S BASEMENT VIDEO BUNKER, SURROUNDED BY ALL HER TECHIE JUNK. SHE WOULDN'T MAKE EYE CONTACT WITH ME.

"WHAT'S THE BIG DEAL ANYWAY?" SHE SAID, STARING BULLETS INTO HER MONITOR. "YOU GUYS WERE OFF DOING YOUR RIVER THING AND I GOT RESTLESS. ALSO YOU BOTH SMELL LIKE THREE DAYS OF CAMPING, AND I MEAN THAT IN A BAD WAY."

FITZ SNIFFED THE AIR IN THE GENERAL LOCATION OF MY SHOULDER AND BACKED UP TWO STEPS.

"VERY FUNNY," I SAID, THEN I LOOKED AT SARAH UNTIL SHE FINALLY CAUGHT MY EYE. "SOMETHING HAPPENED, DIDN'T IT? SOMETHING SCARY."

SHE GOT UP OUT OF HER CHAIR AND WENT TO HER OLD RECORD PLAYER. SHE'D lately been into somber music, and the needle hit side one of Prologue by The Milk Carton Kids. When she turned around, she was white as a ghost.

"Sarah, what is it?" I asked. "We're here now. It's okay."

She came back and we all sat down together near her computer.

"Can I just say that there should be a rule about the Crossbones," she said, getting a little more upset. The slow strum of Michigan, a really sad song, played quietly behind her. "Two thirds of our membership should not be allowed to go off the grid at the same time. At least I had Steve and his snaggletooth to protect me."

She looked like she was about to cry. Okay, big deal alert. Get this thing under control, Ryan McCray.

"I'll talk to my dad," I said. "It won't happen again."

"Or one of us will call in sick if it

does," Fitz added, handing Steve to Sarah for comfort. "No problem."

We looked at each other and let the music play and I took a package of peanut M & M's out of my pocket. I always kept small yellow bags of them in my gear because they didn't melt and they tasted like sweet crunchy bolts of energy on a long float down a river. I tore open the package and poured a third in each of our hands and we ate.

"So what happened?" Fitz asked through a mouthful of peanuts and chocolate and crunchy colored veneer.

"Better if I show you," she said, leaning over towards her laptop and setting up a video. She set the dog on the floor. "I thought if I went in there and asked it some questions I could get some answers before you got back." Sarah's finger was shaking as she went to start the video. Now that I've seen it, I can see why.

You have to see this video! It will shock you. You can't read on until you see what Sarah saw.

The phantom showed itself.

SARAHFINCHER.COM

PASSWORD:

ISLANDOFMADNESS

ENTER THE PHANTOM ROOM

IF YOU DARE.

The sound of sad music from Sarah's record player filled the room after we watched that video. Fitz crunched M and M's nervously, and I tried to imagine how scary it must have been for Sarah.

"Is that for real, or did you doctor it?" I asked. I had to at least be sure. Sarah was good at special effects.

"First you abandon me, now you accuse me of fakery?" she asked. "Very nice."

"Sorry, I'm—It's just so...wow," I said.

"Yeah, wow," Fitz added. He tossed back his last M & M and stared at the floor. When he looked up, he'd made up his mind.

"I believe you, Sarah," he said. Fitz caught my eye and I nodded. "We both do. And this video makes it clear."

"Makes what clear?" she asked, leaning in closer.

Fitz leaned forward and gazed at the monitor.

"I'M THE ONLY ONE MY MOM WILL TALK TO."

FITZ'S WORDS SAT HEAVY IN THE ROOM AND I FELT MY BREATH CATCH IN MY THROAT.

"SO YOU'RE SURE IT WAS HER?" I ASKED.

WE'D ALL SEEN THE BODY IN THE BED AND THE WAY IT HAD MOVED INSIDE THE PHANTOM ROOM (IF YOU DIDN'T SEE THIS, YOU GOTTA WATCH THAT VIDEO!). IF IT HAD BEEN ME INSTEAD OF SARAH IN THAT ROOM MY ARMS WOULD HAVE FLAILED AROUND LIKE A MONKEY. I'D HAVE KNOCKED OVER THE CAMERA AND RAN OUT OF THE ROOM SCREAMING.

"WE COULDN'T REALLY SEE A FACE," SARAH SAID. SHE WAS COMING BACK TO US, LESS UPSET AND MORE TRUSTING.

"IT WAS HER," FITZ SAID WITH CERTAINTY. MAYBE HE JUST WANTED IT TO BE HIS MOM, WHO KNOWS. I GUESS IN THE END IT DIDN'T REALLY MATTER ALL THAT MUCH. WHAT MATTERED WAS WHAT THIS PHANTOM WAS trying to tell us something, and Fitz was the only person it would talk to.

"Can we swing by your place and get cleaned up?" Fitz asked. He looked at the time on a clock shaped like an owl on one of the walls.

We had an hour to kill before 10:07PM.

"Sure, let's do that," I said. "Meet up on Fitz's back porch at 10:00PM?" Everyone nodded. The Crossbones were back together again and ready to get some answers.

But how?

<u>River time</u>

"I did some thinking on the trip," Fitz said as we walked back to his house.

We'd cleaned up fast, raided the fridge for leftover lasagna, and taken slabs of brownies from a pan on the counter with us. I was not surprised that

Fitz had done some thinking on the river, and I was enjoying my brownie, so I let him talk while I ate.

When you're on a river rowing a boat for ten hours a day, it gives you a lot of time to think. The rhythm of the rowing and the rocking of the water has a way of putting you into a trance. This has always been especially true for Fitz, who is on the quiet side to begin with. He loved river time because it was thinking time without any of the normal distractions. No phones, no television or music; just the gentle rocking of the river, driving you downstream at three or four miles per hour.

"We have two really important pieces of information," Fitz began. "One is Karl Snediker. He must be tied to this in one way or another. The other is this word we keep hearing over and over: Sid. At first I thought it was a name, but now I'm not so sure."

"What do you mean?" I asked through a gloppy mouthful of brownie. I needed a glass of milk in the worst way. "Maybe it's an acronym, you know, like each letter stands for a word."

I nodded enthusiastically. The sugar rush had my head buzzing. "S could stand for Sned. I could see that."

"I was thinking the same thing," Fitz said. I got the feeling he had more to say, but we arrived at Sarah's house and she was waiting for us outside with Steve on a leash.

I handed her the part of my brownie that I hadn't eaten.

"Gee, thanks," she said, and popped the one bite into her mouth. I just nodded because I had five times as much as that in my mouth. I was a little bit of a hog when it came to my mom's brownies.

We walked under the light of the moon and listened to the quietness of Skeleton Creek. Not even 10PM and

THE PLACE WAS DISSERTED. IN THE DISTANCE I COULD HEAR THE CREAK RUNNING BY.

"FITZ THINKS SID IS AN ACRONYM," I SAID.

SARAH NODDED. "I THINK HE MIGHT BE RIGHT."

"I'VE GOT SOME QUESTIONS FIGURED OUT," FITZ SAID AS WE APPROACHED HIS HOUSE. "I CAN HANDLE IT. NO PROBLEM."

HE WAS TRYING TO CONVINCE HIMSELF, NOT US, AS HE WIPED A BEAD OF SWEAT FROM HIS BROW AND ATTEMPTED TO STAY CALM. I STILL FELT AS THOUGH FITZ WAS THINKING SOMETHING HE WASN'T SAYING, BUT I DIDN'T WANT TO PRESS HIM TOO HARD. FITZ COULD BE SKITTISH IF HE GOT TOO STRESSED. BETTER TO LET HIM DO THIS ON HIS OWN TERMS AND WITH HIS OWN IDEAS.

"I HOPE IT DOESN'T HAPPEN FOR YOU LIKE IT HAPPENED FOR ME," SARAH SAID. SHE SET THE LAPTOP DOWN AND OPENED IT UP. "I WOULDN'T WISH THAT ON ANYONE."

"SHE'S NOT GOING TO BE LIKE THAT

with me," Fitz said. "I'm sure of it."

The way Fitz was acting, I believed him. He'd been the most calm and levelheaded of the Crossbones since the start, like it really was his mom up there and he had nothing to fear. I had my doubts.

"You guys," Sarah said, concern rising in her voice.

I looked over at her, but it was dark enough I couldn't see what she was having a problem with. Fitz and I both stepped closer and looked down, where Steve was gnawing on the cord leading up to the phantom room. It appeared that this wasn't the first time he'd done this, because he'd chewed all the way through the line.

"How does he do that with one tooth?" Sarah wondered out loud.

"He'd got more teeth than that," Fitz said. "His back row is loaded with teeth."

I bent down and looked at the frayed feed from the phantom room. "He must have been doing this while you were up there in the room last night," I said, glancing up at Sarah. "Looks like he just finished the job."

We all had the same idea at the same time: what time is it?

Phones came out one-two-three and I groaned. "10:02PM. We've only got five minutes. That's not enough time to replace the cord."

"I could fix this one, but it will take longer than we have," Sarah said. "Should we postpone until tomorrow night?"

Fitz was more determined than ever, and who knew? Maybe he'd lose his nerve if we waited another day. I didn't want to influence his decision, so I didn't say anything.

Fitz looked at the door leading into the house and then down at Steve.

"What am I going to do with you, little buddy?" he said.

Steve barked happily and went back to chewing on the cord.

We stood around staring at each other, the house, and the cemetery. Sarah was particularly fidgety and nervous. Usually she could channel her nerves into her work, but without anything to film, she had nothing to do but think about the last time she'd been in that room.

"Don't do it, Fitz," she finally said.

But Fitz was already turning to go and there was no stopping him. He'd set his mind to going back to the phantom room and there was nothing Sarah or anyone else could do to stop him. I understood, as best I could anyway. If it was the ghost of my own mom up there and I had a chance to communicate with her, I'd take it even if there was a risk it might be a scary experience.

"If it looks like there's a body in the bed, don't go in," Sarah said. "I didn't see it until it was too late."

Fitz didn't even look back as he grabbed for the door. A second later, he was gone, swallowed by the darkness on the first floor landing.

"I don't feel good about this," Sarah said. She picked up Steve and petted him rapidly. "And I really don't like that we can't record it. Bugs me."

I understood Sarah at that moment, too. Sometimes, if I couldn't write things down, it was as if they didn't happen and never existed to begin with. It was the same for Sarah. If she couldn't film it, it wasn't real. It had never happened.

"Maybe it's okay this once," I said, mostly trying to kill time waiting for Fitz to come back. "Some things are better left un-recorded."

We waited.

And waited.

It was excruciating.

Looking up at the room, the lights began to flutter.

"What's going on up there?" Sarah asked, terribly worried for Fitz.

Noise poured out of the phantom room, piercing the night with shrieks and wailing.

"Fitz!" I yelled.

The window facing out towards the patio suddenly burst outward, sending tiny shards of glass raining down next to us as the heavy curtains blew outward. I thought it was Fitz, being thrown out of the window, but I saw instead a foggy patch of light exit the room. It swirled in a circle with a darker patch of something unearthly, a black and gray mass of energy wrestling in mid air.

"What's happening, Ryan?!" Sarah yelled.

The noise passed into a warped blanket of sound as the black part of

THE CLOUD WAS SUCKED INTO THE CEMETERY LIKE WATER DOWN A DRAIN.

WHEN I LOOKED AGAIN AT THE WINDOW, THERE WAS NOTHING. NO GRAY OR BLACK FOG, NO SOUND.

SARAH STOOD UP AND CLUTCHED STEVE SO HARD I THOUGHT HIS TOOTH MIGHT POP OUT OF HIS HEAD.

"I'M GOING IN," SHE SAID, SHIVERING WITH FEAR.

"ONLY IF I GO IN WITH YOU," I SAID, EVEN THOUGH IT WAS THE LAST THING I WANTED TO DO.

WE APPROACHED THE DARKENED DOOR AND PEERED INSIDE AT THE SAME MOMENT FITZ CAME RUNNING DOWN THE STAIRS. HE THREW OPEN THE DOOR. I DON'T KNOW IF SARAH SCREAMED, BUT I KNOW I DID. WHEN I CALMED DOWN I FOUND MYSELF STANDING ALL THE WAY OVER BY THE IRON FENCE AT THE EDGE OF THE CEMETERY.

"JUMPY MUCH?" FITZ ASKED.

"YOU SCARED THE PANTS OFF ME!" I

YELLED.

FITZ LOOKED AT MY PANTS IN THAT CALM WAY HE HAS OF LOOKING AT THINGS. "NOPE. YOUR PANTS ARE STILL ON."
I WALKED CAUTIOUSLY BACK TO THE PORCH AND WE ALL STOOD TOGETHER. SARAH AND I PEPPERED FITZ WITH QUESTIONS WITHOUT GIVING HIM SPACE TO ANSWER. ARE YOU OKAY? WHAT HAPPENED IN THERE? WHAT DID YOU FIND OUT? WHAT'S WITH THE WINDOW? AND THE FOG?

"TAKE IT EASY YOU GUYS," FITZ SAID. "I DIDN'T SEE ANY FOG, BUT WHEN THE DOOR SLAMMED SHUT UP THERE, THE WINDOW DID EXPLODE TOWARDS THE CEMETERY. SO THAT WAS SHOCKING."

FITZ SEEMED TO FINALLY GET THAT HE'D JUST HAD AN INSANE PARANORMAL EXPERIENCE AND HAD TO SHAKE HIS HEAD TO GATHER HIMSELF.

HE LOOKED BACK AT US BOTH.

"I'VE GOT GOOD NEWS AND BAD NEWS. WHICH DO YOU WANT FIRST?"

We opted for the good news, because it was dark outside, there was a phantom room nearby, and we were standing next to a cemetery. Bad news could wait.

"I figured out what Sid stands for," Fitz said calmly.

"That's big," Sarah said. "Are you sure?"

"Yeah, I'm sure."

"And I'm going to guess the bad news is what it means, right?" I said. I could read Fitz like a book.

Fitz's face clouded over and he came closer, sitting down at the old picnic table. We sat, too.

"I did the same thing we did before," Fitz began. "I asked the room questions and the room answered."

"What did you ask it?" Sarah wondered, on the edge of her seat.

"First I asked if Sid stood for three words, and the door moved closed a little. That's a yes. I kind of already knew that, and I also knew the first word: Sned. I just knew. But I asked anyway: does the S stand for Sned. And the door moved a little more closed."

"That leaves the I and the D," Sarah said. I could see the wheels turning in her head, trying to come up with what they could stand for.

"The next part seemed kind of basic," Fitz went on. "Sned is. The I stood for is, the door confirmed it."

"Good job, Fitz," I said. "That does make sense. But Sned is what?"

"I didn't know for sure, but I had an idea. So I asked: what is D? The door couldn't answer because it wasn't a yes or no question. But another picture fell off the wall."

"A picture of what?" Sarah asked breathlessly. She was dying to figure this out.

"It was a picture of my mom. So I asked

again: what is D? And another picture fell. It was also of my mom."

I put two and two together. "You're mom isn't alive, right?"

"Right," Fitz said. "So I asked: Is D dead? And that's when the door slammed all the way shut."

Sarah's mouth fell open. "Sned is dead."

"Yeah," Fitz said. "Sned is dead."

"But Roy said—" and before I could finish I swallowed my own words. Roy had said Karl Snediker was alive and well, but the phantom room was telling us Sned was dead.

"This is bad," Sarah said. "Real bad."

"There's one more thing, a very strange thing," Fitz added. "When the door slammed shut, a coin flew out in the room."

"What do you mean a coin?" I asked.

"I know, weird right?" Fitz said. He dug into his pocket and pulled out a coin

THE SIZE OF A FIFTY CENT PIECE. "I PICKED IT UP, THOUGHT IT MIGHT BE IMPORTANT. AT FIRST I THOUGHT OH WELL, THERE WAS A COIN UNDER THE DOOR OR SOMETHING AND THE DOOR SLAMMED SO HARD THE COIN JUMPED OUT TOWARDS ME. BUT NO, THIS IS NO ORDINARY COIN. I THINK THIS COIN CAME FROM SOMEWHERE ELSE."

"YOU MEAN LIKE, FROM ALBUQUERQUE?" SOMETIMES MAKING JOKES MADE ME FEEL BETTER WHEN GHOSTS WERE AROUND.

"NO. I MEAN LIKE FROM OVER THERE."

FITZ POINTED AT THE CEMETERY AND HIS MEANING WAS CLEAR: THE COIN HAD COME FROM OVER THERE. FROM THE DEAD SIDE OF THINGS.

"HOW CAN YOU BE SO SURE?" SARAH ASKED. "LET ME SEE IT."

SARAH TOOK THE COIN, WHICH I COULD TELL WAS HEAVY IN HER HAND, AND LOOKED AT BOTH SIDES.

"TIME OF DEATH, 10:07PM."

I looked at the coin, too, and saw what they'd seen. Time of Death, 10:07PM, etched into the metal.

"This is totally nuts," I said. "What do you think it means?"

None of us had the answer to that question, but Fitz did have an idea we all shared as he gazed out into the cemetery.

"I bet Roy Web could tell us."

I thought about that, and then voiced my very real concern.

"If he doesn't kill us first."

The crypt yard

We should have told someone about what we were doing and all that had happened, but we were the Crossbones, and we were serious about it. We understood that this was our mystery to figure out and no one else's, but it was more than that. It felt to me like if we did tell someone else, what we

WERE DOING WOULDN'T MATTER ANYMORE. OR WORSE, SOME KIND OF DARK POWER WOULD COME AFTER US. A SECRET SOCIETY IS FIRST AND FOREMOST A SECRET. IT LOSES ITS IMPORTANCE ONCE EVERYONE KNOWS ABOUT IT.

SO WE DIDN'T TELL ANYONE.

WALKING INTO THE CEMETERY WAS HARDER THIS TIME THAN THE OTHER TWO TIMES HAD BEEN. BEFORE WE'D HAD NO REASON TO BE REALLY AFRAID. THERE HAD BEEN NO REASON TO WORRY ABOUT ROY WEB. BUT NOW THAT WE'D DECODED A MESSAGE FROM THE DEAD, IT FELT LIKE WE MIGHT NOT MAKE IT BACK OUT ALIVE.

"HE'S NOT HERE," SARAH SAID WHEN WE ARRIVED AT HIS LITTLE SHACK AT THE FAR END OF THE GROUNDS. "WHERE ELSE WOULD HE BE AT THIS HOUR?"

THE HOUR OF WHICH SHE SPOKE WAS TURNING TOWARDS MIDNIGHT AGAIN, THE WORST TIME TO BE STANDING AROUND IN A CEMETERY. I LOOKED TO MY LEFT AND SAW THE

MOONLIGHT CASTING SHADOWS OVER THE HOLE ROY HAD DUG. IT STILL HADN'T BEEN FILLED, AND I WORRIED MORE THAN EVER THAT HE PLANNED TO PUT ALL THREE OF US IN THERE.

"COME ON," FITZ SAID, PULLING STEVE ALONG ON HIS LEASH. "LET'S KEEP SEARCHING. HE HAS TO BE OUT HERE SOMEWHERE."

"MAYBE WE SHOULD JUST GO HOME FOR TONIGHT AND TRY AGAIN WHEN THE SUN COMES UP," I SAID. THIS SEEMED LIKE A VERY REASONABLE PLAN TO ME. "AT LEAST THEN WE'D SEE HIM WHEN HE JUMPS OUT FROM BEHIND A TREE AND ATTACKS US WITH A SHOVEL."

"HE'S GOT A POINT," SARAH SAID. SHE WAS STARTING TO THINK SEARCHING THE GRAVEYARD WAS A BAD IDEA, TOO.

FITZ DIDN'T EVEN STOP TO HEAR US OUT. HE WAS BEING VERY DETERMINED. "YOU GUYS GO HOME IF YOU WANT TO. I'M FINDING ROY WEB."

I'D ALWAYS KNOWN THAT GIVEN THE RIGHT CIRCUMSTANCES FITZ COULD BE AN

EXTRAORDINARILY DETERMINED PERSON. I'VE SEEN HIM CAST A DRY FLY TO THE SAME RISING FISH FOR HOURS WITHOUT A SINGLE BITE. IT SHOULDN'T HAVE SURPRISED ME HE WOULD SEARCH UNTIL ROY WEB WAS FOUND, NO MATTER HOW LONG IT TOOK. THIS WAS MORE PERSONAL FOR HIM THAN IT WAS FOR ME. MAYBE THE IDEA OF WAITING OVERNIGHT WAS TOO MUCH TO IMAGINE.

I GLANCED AT SARAH AND I COULD SEE SHE AGREED. "WAIT UP, WE'RE COMING," I SAID. FITZ SLOWED DOWN UNTIL WE CAME UP BESIDE HIM.

"CROSSBONES TO THE END," SARAH SAID.

"YUP, TO THE END," I AGREED.

WE WALKED THAT GRAVEYARD FOR ALMOST AN HOUR, SEARCHING EVERY CORNER. AFTER AWHILE IT STARTED TO FEEL LIKE WE WERE WALKING IN CIRCLES, PASSING THE SAME TOMBSTONES OVER AND OVER AS WE CAME TO THE DARKEST PART OF THE NIGHT. THE MOON WAS GONE, HIDDEN BEHIND TREES AND CLOUDS. IT WAS STARTING TO FEEL LIKE ROY WAS gone.

"Maybe he knew we were onto him and he left town," Sarah said.

"Or possibly he's visiting a friend or something," I added.

That was when Steve, our tiny dog companion, lost it. He'd had enough of walking around on a leash and being obedient. Steve took off at a full run, barking at full tilt, and the leash slipped through Fitz's fingers.

"As if we don't have enough problems already," Fitz complained. "Give me a break."

"Come on, he's headed for the crypt yard!" Sarah said, and she took off after the dog. We all did.

Did I mention that it was really dark? Because I need an excuse for tripping over a piece of broken tombstone and face planting in a cemetery. Not my proudest moment, and what was worse was no one tried to help

ME OR EVEN ASK IF I WAS INJURED OR DEAD. THEY JUST KEPT ON RUNNING.

"THANKS FOR THE HAND, GUYS. NO REALLY, I'M FINE."

I GOT UP AND FELT EQUALLY EMBARRASSED, AFRAID, AND BUMMED OUT THAT MY FRIENDS HAD DITCHED ME FOR A DOG. THERE WERE PIECES OF GRASS ON MY SHIRT AND I BRUSHED THEM OFF, FEELING LIKE A KID ON A PLAYGROUND WHO'D JUST BEEN KNOCKED DOWN BY A BULLY.

"GUYS?" I SAID SOFTLY. THEN LOUDER: "HEY GUYS!"

NO ONE ANSWERED, SO THAT WAS ALARMING. I WALKED, THEN I RAN, THEN I HOPED I WOULDN'T FALL DOWN AGAIN. THE WALLS OF THE CRYPT YARD LOOMED UP TOWARDS ME LIKE THE SHADOW OF A BUILDING AND I PULLED MY PHONE OUT, CLICKING IT ON FOR SOME FAINT LIGHT. IT WASN'T UNTIL I WALKED AROUND THE CORNER OF THE WALL THAT I SAW THE BIG DOOR SITTING AJAR.

THE CRYPT YARD WAS OPEN.

A barely visible shadow moved across the door and I shoved my phone in my pocket, extinguishing the light.

"Hello?" I ventured quietly. "Roy?"

But no one answered. I crept forward two or three steps and then Sarah jumped out from inside the crypt yard and stood next to the door.

"Hurry up, Ryan! We found something."

For the second time in a few hours I had to check my pants to make sure they hadn't been scared right off my body. I also screamed again, a habit that was starting to feel like a bad mole I'd never get rid of.

I thought about telling her I'd fallen down, but how lame would that have been? So I followed her. Once inside and around a few of the looming fortresses of stone, I saw what they'd found.

"No way," I said.

Fitz was staring down a set of stone steps just like I was. So was Sarah. We were all looking at this gaping mouth of earth and stone wondering what was under the crypt yard.

"I think my dog went down there," Fitz said.

"Bummer," I answered, because honestly, it totally was and my vocabulary seemed to have diminished into one and two word phrases.

The piece of stone that had covered the hole had been slid sideways, disappearing into a slot in a giant above ground crypt.

"This has been here a long time," Sarah said, looking more carefully at how the stone door worked. "And it was definitely planned out. There's a secret room down there, no doubt about it."

"Or maybe there's just a lot of bones," I suggested lamely. "Or it's like

King Tut's tomb and if we go down there we'll be cursed."

"Ryan, you sound like a lunatic," Sarah said. "Try to stay calm."

It was true, I was not usually the calmest of the bunch in situations like this. I was the one who didn't even show up for this part of things. But here I was, watching Sarah and Fitz start down a narrow, steep set of stairs into darkness.

"There's a light," Fitz whispered. "It's faint, but it's down there."

I should have told them I would stand guard at the door in case Roy came back and sealed us underground, but I didn't. Instead I looked behind me once, took a deep breath, and basically dove underwater. That's what it felt like walking down those steps. I didn't think I'd ever come back up again. The ocean of darkness would surround me, I'd suffocate, and the door would grind shut forever.

"GET A HOLD OF YOURSELF, RYAN," I SAID TO MYSELF. "THIS ISN'T AS BAD AS IT SEEMS. THINK ABOUT CANDY. AND UNICORNS. THINK HAPPY THOUGHTS."

I WAS THE LAST ONE TO STAND ON THE DIRT FLOOR OF THE ROOM BENEATH THE CRYPT, AND THIS IS WHAT I SAW:

1) FITZ ON ONE SIDE AND SARAH ON THE OTHER, FLANKING ME AS I STARED INTO THE ROOM.

2) CANDLES. IT WAS THE CANDLES THAT HAD MADE THE SOFT LIGHT WE'D SEEN, AND THERE WERE QUITE A FEW. SEVEN I THINK, SCATTERED AROUND THE ROOM ON A CIRCLING SHELF.

3) ROY WEB, STANDING RIGHT IN FRONT OF US. HE WAS HOLDING STEVE. THE DOG WAS HAPPIER THAN IT HAD BEEN ALL NIGHT.

4) THE WALLS WERE BARREN, NOTHING WAS

ON THEM. THEY WERE MADE OF HARD CLAY OR DIRT AND I WONDERED IF IT HAD BEEN ROY, ONE SHOVEL AT A TIME, WHO HAD DUG A VERY LARGE GRAVE UNDER THE CRYPT.

I COULDN'T SEE WHAT WAS BEHIND ROY WEB, BUT THERE WAS SOMETHING THERE. I COULD FEEL IT IN MY BONES AS ROY TOOK OUT A HANDKERCHIEF AND WIPED HIS BALD HEAD.

HE PUT THE HANDKERCHIEF BACK IN THE POCKET OF HIS OVERALLS AND MOVED SEVERAL SLOW STEPS TO THE LEFT. THAT'S WHEN WE SAW WHAT WAS BEHIND HIS GORILLA SIZED FRAME:

A TABLE WITH FOUR CHAIRS. IN ONE OF THE CHAIR THERE WAS A SKELETON OF A PERSON, SLUMPED ONTO THE TABLE. AND THE STRANGEST PART OF ALL? THE TABLE WAS AN EXACT REPLICA OF THE CRYPT YARD ABOVE. IT LOOKED LIKE A LITTLE CITY, THE CITY OF THE DEAD.

"THAT'S SOME TABLE YOU'VE GOT THERE," I SAID LIKE AN IDIOT.

Roy didn't respond as Sarah edged closer for a better look.

"Is that Karl Snediker?" Fitz asked, staring at the bones slumped onto the table. I couldn't believe he was asking Roy Web, the biggest guy in four counties, a question like that.

Roy nodded slowly.

"We got us some trouble," he said. "And now you in it with me. Come on."

Roy walked back to the table, and I grabbed at Sarah's shirt as she moved a step forward.

"We should leave you guys," I said. "We should leave right now."

But it wouldn't have mattered if I could have stopped Sarah, neither of us would have ran. Fitz was already several steps into the room and there was no way we were leaving him behind.

"Did you kill Karl Snediker?" Fitz asked boldly.

While I waited for Roy's answer, I

wondered how many other people Roy had killed. Were we next? And how were we going to leave if he wouldn't give us our dog back?

"I didn't kill ol' Sned," Roy said. "Wudn' me."

"Then who did?" Fitz asked.

Roy gazed around the room and pet the dog.

"He ain't dead. Not yet."

"Uh, Roy," I stammered.

"He's been gone awhile," Roy went on without letting me continue. "But he's back now. He's here."

I didn't see anybody else in the room, but I did feel something. I thought about the strange fog that had come out of the window at Fitz's house and without thinking I brought up the coin. "Fitz, the coin. From before. Maybe it means something."

"You bring the coin?" Roy asked, and by the even tone of his voice I felt

THAT HE KNEW ABOUT THIS ARTIFACT WE'D BEEN GIVEN.

"YEAH, I BROUGHT IT," FITZ SAID, DIGGING IT OUT OF HIS POCKET.

"WHAT TIME ON THE COIN?" ROY ASKED. HE WAS SO CALM IT WAS DRIVING ME NUTS.

"10:07PM," FITZ SAID.

ROY NODDED AND IF I DIDN'T KNOW BETTER I'D HAVE SAID HE ALMOST SMILED. HE PULLED AN OLD POCKET WATCH OUT OF HIS OVERALLS AND LOOKED AT IT.

"THEN IT'S TIME," HE SAID. "COME ON, SIT DOWN AND LET 'OL ROY TELL YOU WHAT'S WHAT."

WE WERE IN SO DEEP ALREADY IT DIDN'T SEEM LIKE A BIG DEAL WHEN WE ALL AGREED AND SAT AT A STRANGE TABLE WHERE A DEAD MAN'S BONES WERE COLLECTING DUST. ROY DIDN'T SIT. HE WANDERED AROUND THE ROOM WITH STEVE, TALKING.

"I KNEW SNED A LONG TIME, 30 YEARS OR SO. HE WAS NOT A GOOD MAN, NOT A friendly man. But he let me live on the property and do the work and he paid me a little bit. It was alright by me."

"How long has he been, you know, dead?" Sarah asked.

That got a little chuckle out of Roy. "About 10 years, give or take. I kept him underground next to my place for a long time, but when I heard you all talking about Sned, I knew it was time to bring him back down here."

"The hole by your place," Fitz said. "You dug him up?"

This was getting worse by the second.

Roy nodded grimly. "Only the bones left. Takes a few years for things to decompose underground, but nature does its work."

We all sat there for a second, staring at the city of the dead rising off of the table in shadows and stone.

"You were going to tell us what

happened to Karl Snediker," Fitz said.

Roy nodded, looking around the room as if he'd just seen a ghost, and then he went on. "He was trying to communicate with the dead long before I ever met him. I suspect that's why he oversaw so many cemeteries around here. Research, you might say. He was almost 80 when he died. I think he was working on that there table for 50 of those years. Strange fella, ol' Sned."

"I think my mom was trying to tell us something about him," Fitz said. "She's dead, too."

Roy seemed to agree. "It takes one to know one. A dead person I mean. And I'm sorry for your loss."

"It was years ago. I never knew her anyway."

"That's too bad," Roy said. "I have a strong feeling she was a good person."

Fitz shrugged and didn't reply, so Roy went on with his story. "Sned was always working on some incantation or science or both, always searching for a way to speak to the dead. That was his passion, to bridge the gap between life and death. But more'n that, he wanted to control whatever it was that come back."

"He doesn't sound like a very nice man," Sarah said. "He should let them rest in peace."

Roy rolled right over that comment, he was moving now. "Over time, Sned got more and more like a troll. He even started looking like one. He had a terrible slump at the end. Like a Gollum. Sned's heart grew darker and darker. He was obsessed with controlling the dead."

Roy loomed over the table, his head drifting down so he could see all the little roads created by the crypts. "He called this the death slayer. Everything about it is precise. It's a perfect replica of the crypt yard above, a city of the dead carved in stone. And between each of the crypts there's a deep stone pathway, where shadows lurk."

Sarah shivered beside me and I thought I saw something move along one of those narrow roads, like a dark fog drifting through. I noticed for the first time that there were spells, symbols, inscriptions, dates, and prayers carved all around the edge of the death slayer.

"I believe this is a complicated and perfect device, a lifetime in the making, for achieving the very outcome Karl Snediker had in mind," Roy said. "To bring back the dead, to control 'em, to make 'em do his bidding."

"There's no way this is true," Sarah said, ever the skeptic. When she spoke, a cold wind blew past her face, wafting her hair back. We were underground. No wind here.

"Okay, I'm not saying I believe any

of this, but that was definitely weird right there," Sarah said.

Roy glanced around the room warily. "He's here. Ol' Sned is watching."

I felt it, too. Whatever had left Fitz's house from the window was here. It was moving, watching, calculating.

"What Sned finally realized, not long after I met him, was that a trade was required," Roy said.

"What do you mean, a trade?" Fitz asked.

"The only way to make the death slayer work was to switch places with the dead. Someone had to die."

I was starting to understand. Fitz was, too.

"So Karl Snediker died, right here at this table," Fitz said. "And he brought my mom back."

Roy nodded slowly. "I think Sned's death released your mom's ghost back into the world, but I think..."

"What?" Fitz asked, because Roy didn't finish.

"Well, I think ol' Sned is out here, too. I think your mom's trying to put him back where he belongs. You know what time 'ol Sned died? 10:07 in the night. I think your mamma came back right then, too. 10:07."

Roy moved to the empty side of the death slayer and held out his hand. "Let me see the coin."

Fitz still didn't act like he trusted Roy, so he hesitated giving it up. He held it where Roy could see it though.

"Suit yourself," Roy said. "But don't say I didn't warn you."

"What's that supposed to mean?" Sarah asked, standing up as if she'd decided she'd had about enough.

"Only ever seen one time-of-death coin in my life," Roy said. He pointed to the one in Fitz's hand. "That there's the second."

"WHAT ARE YOU TALKING ABOUT, ROY?" SARAH ASKED WITH A SHAKY VOICE.

ROY DUG INTO HIS OWN POCKET AND PULLED OUT A COIN THAT LOOKED JUST LIKE THE ONE FITZ HAD. THE ROOM SHOOK, AS IF THE TREMOR OF A COMING EARTHQUAKE HAD STARTED. THEN IT STOPPED. ONE OF THE CANDLES SITTING ON THE SHELF TOPPLED OVER. AND IN THE SOFT LIGHT I SAW SOMETHING MOVE, A FAINT BUT VERY REAL SHADOW DRIFTED ACROSS THE ROOM AND ONTO THE CEILING, HOLDING ABOVE THE DEATH SLAYER.

"HE AIN'T HAPPY," ROY SAID.

"HOW DO WE MAKE HIM GO AWAY?" SARAH ASKED. "I FEEL LIKE HE'S ABOUT TO COVER US ALL LIKE A WET BLANKET AND WE'RE NEVER GOING TO GET OUT OF HERE ALIVE."

ROY HELD THE DEATH COIN IN HIS HAND, CLOSER TO THE DEATH SLAYER, LIKE HE WAS ABOUT TO PUT A QUARTER INTO A PINBALL MACHINE. "I THINK YOUR MOM FORCED SNED

BACK INTO THIS ROOM, AND NOW THAT SNED IS HERE, ALL I GOT'S TO DO IS—"

ROY FLEW BACKWARDS LIKE A RAG DOLL, SLAMMED AGAINST ONE OF THE WALLS, AND SHOOK HIS HEAD. HE WAS AS STRONG AS AN OX, BUT IT HAD TO HURT.

HE MARCHED FORWARD AS IF A GALE FORCE WIND WAS TRYING TO HOLD HIM BACK. THE UNSEEN FORCE OF KARL SNEDIKER DIDN'T WANT ROY ANYWHERE NEAR THE DEATH SLAYER. ROY WAS THROWN BACK AGAIN, BUT HE KEPT COMING.

"THE DEATH COIN IS A REAL OBJECT CONJURED FROM THE WORLD OF THE DEAD. THIS HERE COIN IN MY HAND, IT'S THE ONE GOT MADE WHEN KARL SNEDIKER DIED. AIN'T IT KARL?!"

I STAYED RIGHT WHERE I WAS, BECAUSE WHERE I WAS PUT ME AS FAR AWAY FROM THE GHOST OF KARL SNEDIKER GOING TO WAR WITH THE BIGGEST GUY I'D EVER SEEN. ROY KEPT TRYING, BUT SNED WAS STRONGER. ROY COULDN'T GET WITHIN FIVE FEET OF THE

TABLE.

"WHAT ARE YOU TRYING TO DO?" I YELLED.

"ACCORDING TO SNED'S FINAL WORDS, THE ONLY WAY TO PUT A PHANTOM BACK INTO ITS CRYPT IS TO PUT A DEATH COIN INTO THE ROUND SLOT ON THE TABLE."

THAT INFORMATION MADE THE PHANTOM OF KARL SNEDIKER EVEN ANGRIER. ROY BASHED UP AGAINST THE FAR WALL AGAIN, AND THIS TIME HE DIDN'T GET UP. HE SAT THERE, HEAVING BREATHS, HOLDING OUT THE COIN.

I TOOK A CLOSER LOOK AT THE DEATH SLAYER, WE ALL DID. FITZ SAW IT FIRST, THE SLOT, LIKE A NARROW SHOOT THE COIN COULD STAND UP IN. I WATCHED AS FITZ REACHED OUT WITH HIS OWN COIN IN HAND AND HELD IT OVER THE SLOT. THE PHANTOM SENSES SOMETHING WAS WRONG AND ITS FOGGY SHADOW MOVED LIQUID AND FAST, KNOCKING FITZ OFF HIS FEET.

"FITZ!" SARAH SCREAMED.

WE WERE NEXT. THE PHANTOM KARL SNEDIKER REARED UP, HIGH TOWARDS THE ceiling, and I could finally make out some ghastly features in the roiling black fog. It looked at me, then at Sarah, and then down at the death slayer.

Fitz had dropped the death coin as he fell backwards and it had begun to roll down into the depths of the city of the dead. It turned as the slot did, carrying it down and down into the chasm of the table.

The phantom made some horrifying sounds and moved back from the table, but it was too late. A small piece of Karl Snediker's ghost had been captured by the death slayer. A thin cable of dark fog was already filling the streets between the crypts, pulling and pulling and pulling. Soon all the pathways between the crypts were teaming with black smoke, taking Karl back to where he'd come from.

All at once the smoke rose into

A PLUME ABOVE THE TABLE AND THEN, LIKE WATER DOWN A DRAIN, IT WAS SUCKED INTO ONE OF THE CRYPT'S IN THE CITY OF THE DEAD.

EVERYTHING WENT QUIET AND STILL.

"I THINK HE'S GONE," SARAH SAID.

ROY STOOD UP SEEMED TO CHECK HIS LIMBS FOR BROKEN BONES. HE WALKED FORWARD, SMILING. "OL' SNED IS BACK WHERE HE BELONGS."

FITZ STOOD UP, TOO, AND CAME OVER TO WHERE WE WERE. "MAN, THAT WAS SERIOUSLY MESSED UP."

"YOU SAID IT BRO," I ADDED. THE CROSSBONES HAD FINALLY PUT A REAL PHANTOM BACK IN ITS PLACE. IT WAS SCARY, BUT IT WAS ALSO INCREDIBLY COOL.

ROY HELD THE DEATH COIN IN HIS HAND OUT TOWARDS FITZ. "THIS HERE IS YOUR COIN NOW. I THINK THERE'S SOMEONE READY TO REST IN PEACE, BUT SHE'S NOT HERE. SHE FORCED KARL BACK IN HERE, BUT I DON'T THINK SHE'S AROUND."

FITZ TOOK THE COIN. "I KNOW WHERE TO FIND HER. THANKS, ROY. THANKS FOR EVERYTHING."

ROY HAD A SUDDEN, STRICKEN LOOK ON HIS FACE. "WHERE'S STEVE?!"

IN ALL THE COMMOTION, STEVE HAD BEEN THE LAST THING EVERYONE WAS THINKING ABOUT. NOW WE ALL CALLED FOR HIM AND HE SLOWLY EMERGED FROM A DARK CORNER, SCARED AND SHIVERING, DRAGGING HIS LEASH BEHIND HIM. THE ONLY DOG IN THE WORLD TO SEE A GHOST WAS GLAD IT WAS OVER.

FITZ CALLED STEVE OVER, BUT THE LITTLE DOG WENT RIGHT TO ROY INSTEAD, SO ROY PICKED HIM UP. HE GAVE STEVE A GOOD SCRATCH, THEN HELD HIM OUT TOWARDS FITZ.

"I ONLY GOT STEVE A FEW DAYS AGO," FITZ SAID. "I THINK YOU SHOULD KEEP HIM. HE LIKES YOU, AND YOU NEED A FRIEND OUT HERE. I MEAN, YOU'VE GOT US NOW. BUT YOU KNOW, FOR WHEN IT'S LATE AND NO ONE IS around."

Roy lit up like Fourth of July. He was like a big kid, happier than I'd ever seen him before. He didn't say anything, just nodded, and we all filed out into the night.

Once more into the phantom room

The next night we all met up again at Fitz's house. Earlier in the day Sarah had replaced the cord Steve had chewed through, and when Fitz and I arrived she was already testing the feed.

"We're good to go," she said. "But are you sure you want to go in there again?"

Sarah seemed mildly shaken, still recovering from the night before. It was the strangest night of our lives, and we'd lived to see another day. I think we were all feeling a little nervous about life in general and where it was going to lead for the Crossbones.

"Mind if we join you for the show?"

We all whirled around and saw Roy standing there. Steve was on the ground obediently walking out of the cemetery without a leash.

"You trained him fast," I said.

"Keep him away from the equipment and you can stay," Sarah said as she smiled. I was glad Roy and Steve had shown up. It made everything feel safer.

Fitz hadn't talked much over breakfast or at work all day. He'd stayed to himself, and I let him be alone with his thoughts. Even now, standing in front of the house, he seemed distant.

"You okay, Fitz?" I asked. I thought about putting a hand on his shoulder as he stared at the house, but then I remembered the phantom of Karl Snediker and thought it might freak Fitz out.

He turned to us and sighed. I thought he was gathering his courage,

BUT IT TURNED OUT HE HAD SOMETHING TO SAY UNRELATED TO GOING BACK INSIDE THE PHANTOM ROOM. "I WENT BY THE TRAILER LAST NIGHT AND MY DAD WAS THERE. HE'S BACK. SEEMED FINE, QUIET AS USUAL. I DIDN'T TELL HIM ANYTHING ABOUT ANY OF THIS AND I'M NOT GOING TO."

FITZ LOOKED AT ROY WEB. "ROY, I THINK YOU SHOULD BE A MEMBER OF OUR SECRET SOCIETY, THE CROSSBONES. I THINK YOU ALREADY KNOW WHAT WE DO."

ROY HAD A LOOK ON HIS FACE THAT MADE ME THINK IT HAD BEEN A LONG TIME SINCE HE'D HAD A FAMILY OF HIS OWN. AND MAYBE IN SOME WAYS, THIS WAS THE BIGGEST THING THE CROSSBONES COULD DO: GIVE A LONELY PERSON A HOME. AND THERE WAS THE OBVIOUS BONUS OF HAVING A HUGE GUY WATCHING OUR BACKS. I HOPED HE'D SAY YES.

"BEEN A GOOD WEEK FOR OL' ROY," HE SAID. "I GOT ME A DOG AND A BUNCH OF FRIENDS. I ACCEPT."

FITZ BEAMED. FOR THE FIRST TIME IN

awhile he seemed genuinely happy.

"It's 10:05," Sarah said, bringing everyone back to reality. "You really want to do this?"

"Yeah, I need too," Fitz said, glancing up at the blown out window to the phantom room. "I need to hear from her one more time."

Fitz walked right into the house, no hesitation, and we all gathered around Sarah's laptop. We waited until 10:07PM, and then something happened in the phantom room.

You need to see it. And when you do, make sure you look at the ceiling in the room right at the end. Something is there.

Something that should not be there.

Don't read the end until you see the last video!

SARAHFINCHER.COM

PASSWORD:

NIGHTVALE

ENTER THE PHANTOM ROOM

IF YOU DARE.

Fitz's mom goes home

We all sat around the picnic table. Well, all but Roy. He was too big. Roy looked at the house and the window and then out to the cemetery.

"She's gone," he said. "I think she's under the crypt yard."

Fitz nodded. He held a folded up letter in his hand. "Yeah, she's definitely gone. I could feel the room emptying out after the last book fell."

"Are you going to read it?" Sarah asked.

"Already did," Fitz told us, and it made more sense then why it had taken him so long to come out of the house. He'd retrieved the book that was stuck to the ceiling, that much we'd seen on the video feed. But what we hadn't known then was that a letter was tucked away inside the book. It was a letter Fitz's mom had written to him before he was even born. At least that's what Fitz told us. Anyway, it was personal, and with Fitz, that meant he wasn't going to show it to us.

"I feel better," he said. "She loved me. I can see that now. And she never had a chance to tell me some things before she, you know."

Yeah, we knew.

Fitz still had the death coin and he set it on the table. "Would you do this for me, Roy? She'll go back willingly. She's not going to give you any trouble. She did all she came to do."

Roy picked up the coin. "Rest in peace, you got it."

We stuck around for a little longer, but it felt like we were supposed to go off in our own directions and take a break from Crossbones work. Soon enough we'd be together again, in a day or two, finding some other mystery to solve in Skeleton Creek.

But for now we watched as Roy and

Steve wandered out into the cemetery like a four legged ghost. I watched Fitz walk into his house, where he would sleep peacefully for the first time in forever.

"See you tomorrow?" Sarah asked when it was just us two again. It always came down to the two of us, and I was happy about that.

"Yeah, tomorrow," I said. "I have a feeling we're going to stumble into something else before too long."

"Speaking of stumbling into things," she said.

And then she started telling me about another dredge only 20 miles down the road and how there were a lot of rumors about it. She told me about the ghost town that surrounded it, how hardly anyone lived up there at all. As I walked down the darkened streets of Skeleton Creek, I knew our work as the Crossbones had only just begun.